Pool Girls

by Cassie Waters

Heat Wave

Simon Spotlight
New York London Toronto Sydney New Delhi

SIMON SPOTLIGHT
An imprint of Simon & Schuster Children's Publishing Division
1230 Avenue of the Americas, New York, New York 10020

Text by Sarah Albee
For information about special discounts for bulk purchases, please contact Simon & Schuster Special Sales at 1-866-506-1949 or business@simonandschuster.com.
Manufactured in the United States of America 0512 OFF
First Edition 10 9 8 7 6 5 4 3 2 1
ISBN 978-1-4424-4146-0 (pbk)
ISBN 978-1-4424-5376-0 (hc)
ISBN 978-1-4424-4147-7 (eBook)
Library of Congress Catalog Card Number 2011935850

Chapter One

"Don't move."

Christina's eyes flew open. Standing right in front of her was Mike Morris. His broad, muscular frame blocked the sun, which made him look as though he were bathed on all sides by a glowing light. She could feel Lindsay and Ashley, who were lying on either side of her, stop breathing as Mike took a gentle step toward her.

Did he want to memorize the way she looked, lounging back on the chair in her new electric-blue bikini, her dark hair piled carelessly on top of her head?

With a quick whisk of his hand across her forearm, he stepped back again and grinned. "Bee," he said.

"Be what?" asked Christina, giggling.

"I think it was a yellow jacket, actually," Mike continued, ignoring Christina's misunderstanding. "Crawling right on your arm. They love soda, so look before you take a sip. Those suckers really hurt when they sting, especially on your tongue."

She barely had time to stammer out a thanks before he turned and walked away. All three girls sat up and watched him walk to the other side of the pool, where the snack-bar staff had just fired up the grill. He joined a group of swim-team guys who were scarfing down chips and dip.

"He is definitely superhot," said Ashley. "I can see why you wanted to join this swim club."

"Totally," agreed Lindsay.

"I wonder if he's part fish," mused Christina. "Maybe that's why he never notices me. He would rather be swimming in the dumb pool than anything else."

"Speaking of hot, it's hot," said Ashley, pulling her hair up into a flawless ponytail. "Ugh. I'm all sweaty. But thanks for having us as your guests today! This looks like an awesome Fourth of July picnic!"

"Yeah, if your invite hadn't come through, I'd be spending the day at my aunt and uncle's house, listening to my aunt brag about how brilliant my cousins are," said Lindsay, rolling her eyes.

"I heard Marty at the snack bar say this was the hottest Fourth of July picnic he's ever organized. And he's been working here for forever," said Christina.

"Look, there's Veronica," muttered Lindsay. "Shocker. She's hanging out with the swim team. Again."

Christina's eyebrows went up. "I thought you guys were really good friends with Veronica."

"'Were' is right," sniffed Ashley. "She's become obsessed with the swim team. It's 'swim team this, practice that, Coach Dana blah-blah-blah.' She never has time for doing important stuff with us."

Christina suppressed a smile. She hadn't been friends with Lindsay and Ashley for very long, but her impression was that they didn't actually do a lot of "important stuff"—at least not that she'd observed. They seemed to spend most of their time shopping, texting, and surfing the Net. At least Veronica, who was also a member of this super-popular group, seemed to care about getting good grades. But Christina wasn't about to complain. This past school year her friendships with her old best friends, Grace Davis and Mel Levy, were totally strained. Grace and Mel just seemed a little immature. Christina was trying to help them grow up, but they didn't seem to like that. So Christina was happy to have these new friends and to be accepted as part of their group. "Yeah, Grace is totally all about the swim team," added Christina. "It's like it sucks you in."

"I'm going to dangle my legs in the water," said Ashley, swinging around and standing up.

"You're not going in?" asked Christina.

"No, I'm having too good a hair day to get it wet," said Ashley, tossing her glossy ponytail this way and that.

"I'll come too," said Lindsay, standing up and joining Ashley.

Behind her dark glasses, Christina sized up their bathing suits. Lindsay's two-piece was a really cool coral color, and Ashley's suit was lavender with pale yellow polka dots. She darted a glance down at her own suit. Were bright colors out of fashion now? Was this so last summer?

"Coming?" asked Ashley.

"Nah, go ahead. I'm just going to lie here and think about how to get Mike Morris to notice me," said Christina, fanning herself with Lindsay's copy of *Teen Vogue* and looking across the pool at Mike over the top of her sunglasses.

"Okay, save us a seat if you go for food," said Lindsay, and the two headed off to the water.

A group of girls from the swim team walked up to the snack table. Christina saw her old friend Grace nudge Mike Morris and say something. They both laughed. Christina gaped. How long had Grace and Mike been so chummy? And since when was Grace that comfortable around boys? She'd always been so painfully shy. Grace had barely spoken to her all summer. Was she mad that Christina had joined the club too? Christina sighed. She and Grace had known each other since preschool. It was sad how people could change so much. Christina had tried so hard, both subtly and not so subtly, to help Grace grow up a bit, to add sophistication to her look. She had offered several times to take Grace under her fashion wing and consult with her about clothing and makeup, but Grace had been so sensitive about it. Christina eyed Grace's wet ponytail, casual T-shirt, and baggy shorts and sighed. Hopeless. Grace might be enjoying her new popularity at RSC, but she still had no fashion sense.

"Hey! You hungry?" Christina heard a cheerful voice behind her.

Christina turned, saw who it was, and smiled. It was Jen Cho, her new-but-not-new friend. They had lived on the same block most of their lives, but they lost touch when Jen went off to Shipton Academy for middle school. But once they discovered they both belonged to RSC, their friendship blossomed again. And being friends with Jen definitely made Christina look good, especially around all those cliquey swim-team girls.

"I'm starved!" said Christina, grabbing her shorts. She pulled them on and stood up. The heat made her feel a little dizzy, and the air rippled above the hot pool deck.

"You shouldn't lie out in the sun like that," said Jen, shaking her head. "Not good for you."

"Yeah, I know," Christina said with a shrug. "But it's too hot to do anything else, even swim!"

Jen laughed. "Well, now both the boys' and girls' swim teams are here, so you'd better get some food before they eat it all! Swimming makes us famished!"

"Hey, girls, can you give me a hand here?" called Coach Dana. She was standing next to three long metal tables that were folded up and propped against the snack bar. "Marty thinks we'll need a few more tables set up. Here, Jen, help me carry this one over."

While Jen and Coach Dana carried off one of the tables, Christina looked around for another person to help her. And there was Mike, not five feet away.

"Hey, a little help?" she called to him.

He turned and trotted over. The two of them lifted the table. Christina admired Mike's arm muscles as he hoisted the other end of the table. He carried it so easily, as though it weighed nothing. "Thanks," said Christina as Mike set it up next to the one Dana and Jen had carried. She searched for something else to say. "So, hot enough for you? My mom told me that the weatherman says he has no idea when this heat wave will break."

"I don't mind the heat," said Mike. "Good excuse to go swimming again!" He gave her a melt-your-heart sideways grin and loped away.

Christina sighed. Why, oh why, did he not seem the least bit interested in her? Did he have a girlfriend? Impossible. She'd have heard through the grapevine if he did. She crossed her arms and let out another sigh.

"Not worth it," someone whispered in her ear.

She whirled around to see Jen again, grinning this time. "What's not worth it?"

"Aw, come on. Any dope can see you're into him. Trust me: he's an okay guy and all, but the only thing Mike Morris cares about is swimming. And that's saying something, coming from me." Jen turned and followed after Coach Dana, who was waiting for help with the next table.

There's got to be some way to get his attention, Christina thought. Her gaze came to rest on Coach Dana, then traveled across the patio area to where the boys' coach, Paul, was standing, grilling hot dogs, and cracking jokes with everyone who passed by. "Hmm," Christina said quietly to herself. "I wonder if *he* has a girlfriend." He was definitely cute, and just the right age for Coach Dana. Christina guessed that he was in college. He looked to be about the same age as Cameron, Grace's brother. Spiky brown hair; medium height; nice, muscular arms. The guys on the swim team all seemed to like him a lot. He struck Christina as a little intense about coaching, but then, so was Dana. Yes, Coach Dana could certainly do worse.

She turned toward Dana, drumming her fingers thoughtfully on her cheek. Definitely attractive, and maybe Paul's age or a year or two younger. *It would be nice if she paid a little more attention to her hair,* Christina thought, but that was a small detail that could be worked out.

This could be a project. A project for her and Mike!

Christina made her way over to Mike, who was talking to Coach Paul about split times, whatever those were, as Paul piled blackened hot dogs onto a plate. She sidled up to Mike and tapped him gently on the arm. "Pssst," she said. "I just had an idea. Got a second?"

Looking slightly baffled, Mike followed her over to one of the still-empty tables. "What's up?" he asked as they sat down.

"I was thinking," she said slowly, taking a second or two for a dramatic pause, so his curiosity might grow. "I was thinking that Coach Paul and Coach Dana might make a good couple. What do you think?"

"Couple? Like, you think they're into each other?"

"Well, no, not yet," said Christina quickly. "That would be our job. To get them together. They both seem so obsessed with coaching and stuff, neither one seems to have noticed that they'd be perfect for each other!"

Mike scratched his head, still looking puzzled. "Why do you think they need to get together?"

Christina sighed. "Does he strike you as rather intense about swimming?"

Mike nodded. "Of course. Is that a bad thing?"

Christina nodded. "It's because he has no life outside of coaching. And neither does she. You can't live on swimming alone."

"You can't?"

"No. You can't. Once they realize they need each other, their lives will be complete. Don't you see? And anyway, it would be fun, like a summer project. For us. To do. . . ." She trailed off and then resolved to try again. "Do you know if Paul has a girlfriend?"

Mike shrugged. "Not sure. I *think* so, but we don't really talk about that stuff."

Boys could be so exasperating. How could he not

know? Mike and Coach Paul spent hours together every day! "Well, find out, will you? Because if he doesn't, we can think of a way to get them together."

"Okay, sure," said Mike. "Good luck with that. Right now I smell cheeseburgers, and they're calling my name." He winked, gave her another half smile, and headed toward the grill area.

Christina watched him go. That was the longest conversation they'd ever had. Even if he didn't seem to get it, she was not going to give up on this scheme. She knew nothing about swimming, but she had excellent people skills. This matchmaking plan was almost too easy—the coaches were *perfect* for each other. And it would give her more reasons to talk to Mike. Once she got things up and running between the two coaches, Mike would see how cool it was to be in a relationship. It might turn his own thoughts to love . . . and she'd be there waiting for him when it finally dawned on him that she, Christina, was perfect for him.

Chapter Two

Grace stood near the snack bar listening to Veronica Massey and Lisa Lehner chat about the swim meet a week from Friday. The meet was a really big one—five other teams from local swim clubs would be coming to RSC, including RSC's arch rival, Fair Isle Swim Club. She looked across the pool to where Christina Cooper was lounging alongside Ashley Karcher and Lindsay Petrarca. Grace sighed. Sometimes she really missed hanging out with her old friend. They'd grown apart over the school year, but ever since they discovered they'd both joined RSC, they'd been seeing each other pretty regularly again. But Grace had become so busy with the swimming and diving teams, and with making new friends at RSC, that they didn't talk much. For the first time in a long time, Grace felt like she belonged someplace, and she felt accepted. All those years of gymnastics had finally paid off. She'd grown too tall to be a competitive gymnast, but the skills she'd acquired helped her become a pretty good diver. She looked back at Christina. Christina had changed so much over the past year. All she cared about was being in the popular crowd at Lincoln Middle School where they both went. That and boys.

Grace watched Mike Morris approach Christina's chair, stoop down, and brush his hand across Christina's arm. Was he moving aside a stray lock of her hair? Her long, brown, glossy, and perfect hair? Hmm, no. She was wearing it up. Whatever. Grace heard Christina laugh. Ugh. She was *such* a flirt!

"Chip?" she heard someone say.

She turned. Justin McGee. It was always Justin. Never Mike. Justin was her age, but she'd never met him before this summer. He was actually from the next town over, but his family belonged to RSC, rather than Fair Isle Swim Club, which was closer to his house. He could be pretty dorky, she had to admit, though he was a tiny bit cute, too. He wasn't Mike-cute, but he wasn't bad if you didn't mind not-very-tall and ears that stuck out a little and hair that grew up instead of down. And also, Justin and Mike were teammates and seemed to hang out together a lot. So Grace figured it was a good idea for her to be friends with Justin, too. "No, thanks," she said. "I'm waiting for them to start grilling up the burgers and dogs."

"How's the swimming going?" asked Justin.

"Okay, not great," said Grace, looking around to see who everyone was starting to sit with at the picnic. "I can't seem to get my arms and legs in sync when I do the backstroke, and forget about the butterfly. Luckily, Coach Dana appreciates how much I stink at those events, so she lets me concentrate on diving."

"You're an awesome diver," said Justin. "I saw you in practice yesterday."

Grace thrilled with pleasure and felt the customary flush zoom to her cheeks. No doubt her face had turned beet red. "Thanks," she said. "I'm still learning, but my gymnastics background helps a lot. Coach Michelle is really nice."

Suddenly Mike Morris was standing next to them. "Hey! Food here yet?" he asked.

"I know. I'm starving," Grace added.

Justin gestured toward the grill stations. "If you want my advice, have one of Marty's burgers, not one of Coach Paul's charred hot dogs. He burns everything. He may be a good coach, but he's a lousy cook."

Mike chuckled. "Totally."

Grace smiled.

"Have a chip," said Justin. He offered Mike the bowl, and Mike took a sizable handful. The two boys started talking about the big meet next week, and Grace's mind wandered.

"Hey, a little help?" they heard someone call. It was Christina. Grace felt her whole body clench up.

Mike hurried away from them to help Christina move a table. Grace and Justin remained standing there, slightly awkwardly. Luckily Coach Dana broke the uncomfortable silence. "Take this," she said, thrusting a tube of sunblock into Grace's hand as she and Jen Cho staggered past with a table. "Slather yourselves. Remember, you have to reapply after you swim."

"But it's getting to be late afternoon," Grace protested.

"Doesn't matter." Coach Dana had a way of being bossy that made Grace like her even more.

Grace and Justin both grinned. "It's nice to know she cares," Grace said with a shrug. All the chairs had been moved to the patio for the picnic, so she sat down on the pool deck and squeezed some sunblock onto her finger. Then she handed it to Justin, who sat down next to her.

Out of the corner of her eye, Grace could see Christina and Mike sitting at an empty table. Christina was smiling and leaning toward Mike, definitely doing her flirty thing.

"So Coach Paul asked me to dive at the meet," said Justin, his voice breaking into Grace's thoughts.

"Oh!" she said, turning to him. "I didn't know you were a diver."

"I'm not," he said. "But Andrew Parker's going to be on vacation next week, so they need an extra diver. I only know four dives, though, so I have a week to learn two new ones. Don't suppose you can help me out a little after practice one of these days?"

"Oh yeah, sure," said Grace vaguely.

"They're saying ten more minutes till food is ready," groaned Mike, plopping down next to them on the pool deck. "Lifting plus swimming always makes me starved."

Grace couldn't think of anything to say. She was used to being near Mike, now that they saw each other so often. But even so, she felt her throat go dry and her breathing get shallow. He was just so good-looking!

Justin broke the silence. "It sure is hot," he said.

"Yeah," agreed Grace, grateful to Justin for coming up with something to say. "If it were any hotter, Marty wouldn't need to turn on the grills. He could just cook the burgers right on the concrete on the pool deck."

Mike wrinkled his brow. "I don't think it could ever get *that* hot," he said.

Justin rolled his eyes. "That was a *joke*, Mike."

The three sat in silence until finally Justin came up with something else to say.

"So I hear you're an awesome artist," he said to Grace.

Grace shrugged. "I like to draw. I'm not, like, great or anything." She knew she had to say something to carry her end of the conversation. But what? She was still so awkward when it came to talking to guys. Suddenly it came to her. "Want me to draw you?" she blurted out to Justin.

Justin looked alarmed. "No!" he said quickly.

Grace drooped. So much for flirting. *That* had backfired.

"Um, I mean, draw him!" said Justin, pointing at Mike.

Mike's eyebrows shot up. "She doesn't have a pencil," he pointed out.

Grace grinned, relieved that they seemed interested. "Here, watch this." She squeezed a goopy dollop of sunblock onto the smooth tiled area that ran alongside the rougher surface of the pool deck. She looked straight into Mike's melting green eyes for a moment, and his gaze locked with hers. She could never, ever have gotten up the gumption to stare at him this way if not for her confidence in her own drawing ability. A ripple of electricity shot through her, but she kept her cool. With her index finger, she smeared the sunblock around into an oval shape, then quickly sketched out the features of Mike's face. She'd always loved finger painting as a kid, and this was just like it.

"Awesome!" said Justin, leaning over and staring down at the likeness, then up at Mike's face. "You got the shape of his eyes, the hair, the whole thing! It really looks like him!"

Mike, who had been staring straight at Grace, now looked down at his image and grinned his sideways grin. "Way awesome," he said. "You're really good."

A giggle escaped Grace, a really stupid-sounding giggle, but the boys didn't seem to care. Maybe she was really learning this hidden art of flirting after all!

"Food's ready!" yelled Coach Paul from over by the grill.

The two boys leaped to their feet and raced toward the grill. Still enjoying her happy reverie, Grace absently pulled a crumpled but clean napkin from her shorts pocket and wiped up the worst of the gloppy white smear. Then she hopped up, dropped it into a trash can, and went to join the gang of kids getting burgers and hot dogs.

Grace was famished, as usual, because swimming had that effect. She headed over to Coach Paul's grilled hot dogs to check them out.

"Hi, Grace," he said, grinning. "Hey, you looked pretty good out there at practice on Friday. I saw you win that sprint in the fly."

Grace grinned, covering her braces. "Thanks," she said shyly. "But I just had a lucky start. Diving is more my thing, I think. I'm working on a back somersault in a tuck position."

"Good for you," he said, then gestured with his spatula toward the heap of hot dogs. "What you need is some protein."

Grace giggled as she looked down at the half-charred, shriveled hot dogs. Justin was right. "I think I'll go for one of Marty's burgers, but thanks."

As she headed toward the burger table, she heard him call after her, "What? You saying I can't grill? I'm practically a professional! Aw, Grace, you really know how to hurt a guy's feelings! You better have some of my soon-to-be-world-famous potato salad, at least!"

Still giggling, she piled her plate with a cheeseburger, chips, green salad, and potato salad, and joined Veronica and Lisa and several other girls from the team. "Coach Paul is funny," she said as she sat down.

"He really is a riot," said Lisa. "I always hear the boys cracking up during practice."

"So we were talking about the medley relay," Veronica

said to Grace. "Lisa says Celine is swimming backstroke."

Lisa nodded. "From Fair Isle. She's good."

"So are you, though," Grace said to Veronica. "No one can beat you."

Veronica shook her head. "RSC has never beaten Fair Isle in the medley relay. Celine is awesome. So is Ellie Aziz, their anchor."

Grace had learned early on that Fair Isle Swim Club was RSC's arch rival. She'd been hearing about how great their diving team was ever since she joined RSC.

"Are you swimming in any heats?" Lisa asked Grace.

Grace shook her head. "No way. Just diving. Coach Dana knows better than to enter me in a swim event!"

Lisa grinned. "Well, we're so glad you're diving for us. I watched you do that reverse dive with the half twist the other day and you looked awesome."

Grace flushed with pleasure. "I was working on that with Coach Michelle on the trampoline," she said. "I'm still trying to nail it."

"Check out Coach Paul over there," said Veronica.

The girls turned to see Paul fanning away billowing black smoke from the grill, coughing. They all laughed.

"Nice guy, but he sure can't cook," said Lisa. "Marty told me Paul brought some potato salad for the picnic and

Marty had to secretly make a new batch because the potatoes were only half-cooked."

A few minutes later Grace was licking the relish and mustard off her fingers when she heard a scream. Veronica and Lisa, who were sitting across the table from her, looked past her and leaped to their feet at almost the exact same time. Horror was written across their faces. Grace whirled around.

Jen Cho, the star swimmer on the junior girls' team, lay sprawled on the pool deck. With a high-pitched squeak, she sat up and grabbed her ankle, then began rocking back and forth as though in awful pain.

"Oh no," said Veronica quietly. "She just wiped out. I saw her do it. I think it's her leg."

A terrible chill ran down Grace's spine, then seemed to twine through the rest of her, turning her to stone. Had Jen just slipped on the greasy patch of sunblock that she, Grace, had not properly cleaned up? Grace half stood up to look over at Jen, but now her legs felt suddenly weak, and she sat down heavily in her chair.

Jen had wiped out right near the spot where Grace had been "drawing" with sunblock. She watched in horror as Coach Dana hurried over to help Jen, followed by Coach Paul and several other members of the girls' team. Dana and Paul helped her stand up, an arm around each of their shoulders. Leaning heavily on the coaches, her tear-stained face glinting in the late-afternoon sunlight, Jen hopped on one foot over to a lounge chair, where they gently settled her into it.

"I'll call her parents," Grace heard Paul say to Dana.

"I'll run and get my car and drive it to the side entrance," she heard Dana say to him.

"Oh, poor Jen," murmured Veronica. "It looks bad."

Grace watched as Christina strode over to the site of the accident and gathered up Jen's bag and flip-flops. She went over to where Jen lay, white-faced and in obvious pain, and sat down next to her. Grace watched Christina smooth Jen's hair and talk quietly to her while Dana came hurrying up to them. Together, Christina and Dana helped Jen hop to the exit and out to Dana's car.

Most of the other kids started talking quietly. Grace was still too horrified to say anything.

"I hope her leg's not too bad," said Lisa, shaking her head. "We can't afford to lose our best swimmer one week from the big meet."

"And she's so nice!" added Veronica. "She's always so upbeat and encouraging before the relay. I don't know how I could ever swim it without her as our anchor!"

Grace tried to swallow, but it felt like she had a tight collar closing off her throat. "Bathroom," she croaked out, standing up. "Be right back."

She walked on unsteady legs into the locker room and sat down on a bench. Her phone buzzed. Through blurred vision, she saw that it was a text from Mel, who was away at her beach house for the summer.

Happy 4th! Another perfect beach day. Family driving me crazy but some gr8 looking guys playing volleyball about twenty feet from my blanket. How R U?

Seeing Mel's message made Grace miss her more than ever. But how could she even begin to tell her what she'd done? No, better not to get into it. She texted back:

Awesome. Big meet a week from Friday. Diving going gr8!!

As soon as she hit send, she buried her face in her hands. What had she done to Jen? Grace felt like she might throw up.

"Hey, what's up? You feeling okay?"

Grace looked up quickly. It was Jaci, her friend from

school. The one who had introduced her to RSC. Jaci was not on the swim team and didn't seem to care what crowd she belonged to. She was dressed for tennis and carrying a racket and a water bottle. Her face was a little flushed and her glasses were steamed up, like she'd just finished an intense game. She peered at Grace, took off her glasses to clean them on her shirt, and put them back on.

"Your face. It looks a little greenish."

"I'm fine," Grace lied. She couldn't tell Jaci the truth. That she'd been flirting with two boys at the same time? That she'd left a slippery spot on the pool deck and that Jen had slipped and possibly really hurt herself? "I think I ate a few too many chips. My stomach hurts," she added weakly.

"Oh, well, I just finished my first and last tennis lesson ever," said Jaci. "My mom's instructor agreed to give me a lesson even though it's Fourth of July. She probably paid him triple overtime. But I'm a hopeless case. I kept hitting the ball over the fence into the golf course."

Grace couldn't say anything. She just nodded.

"I was going to stick around and watch the fireworks. Are you staying?"

"I think I better head home," said Grace. She just couldn't go out there and face Mike and Justin. Were they telling everyone she'd caused the accident? Would they ever speak to her again? She pulled out her phone and texted her mom.

"Okay," said Jaci, looking at her quizzically. "Hey, did I hear someone scream earlier? What was that about?"

"Jen Cho," Grace said in a wooden voice. "She fell and hurt her leg. They took her to the hospital."

Jaci whistled. "Isn't she, like, the star of the swim team?"

Grace gave a tiny nod. "Yep."

"You sure you're okay?"

Grace nodded again and stood up. "I'll see you tomorrow, probably," she mumbled, and hurried out, her eyes blurred with tears.

Chapter Three

"Do you think it's broken?" Jen whispered to Christina. They were both in the backseat of Coach Dana's car, on the way to the hospital. Christina had volunteered to come along, after making sure her mom knew where she was going and that Lindsay and Ashley had a ride home from RSC.

Jen was sitting at an awkward diagonal directly behind the driver's seat, her injured right foot propped on top of tote bags and a folded blanket, which Christina had piled into her own lap. Christina held an ice pack in place on Jen's ankle. She darted a glance at Coach Dana at the wheel. Dana's expression was grim.

"It might be," she admitted. "But it might be fine." She

smiled and readjusted the ice pack. "They'll fix you up. You'll be back in the pool in no time."

Jen's parents were waiting for them at the ER. They helped Jen into a wheelchair and hurried her inside. Christina sat with Jen while her parents and Dana talked at the nurses' desk. In the waiting area sat a mother holding a sleeping baby, a middle-aged man with gauze wrapped around his thumb, and a kid about ten years old with a big scrape down the side of his leg. He was slumped between his parents, a skateboard helmet propped on his lap.

Christina took out her MP3 player and found her yoga playlist. She handed it over to Jen. "Here," she said. "This is a nice, soothing track. It will help you destress."

Jen smiled and took the headphones. "Thanks for waiting with me," she said in a quivery voice.

"Does it hurt a lot?"

Jen nodded, her eyes shiny with tears.

An orderly finally appeared and wheeled Jen away through the double doors to get X-rays, and her parents followed. Dana came over to join Christina in the waiting area. "I can't tell for sure," she said, "but if I had to bet, I'd say it was a fracture."

Christina groaned. "That's terrible. Poor Jen. With the big meet coming up next week too!"

"Come on, I'll take you home," said Dana. "Mrs. Cho said she'd call me when they get home."

As they drove, Christina saw something flash in the sky outside the car window. "Fireworks!" she said. "They must be right over RSC!"

Dana pulled into the parking lot of a closed electronics store and turned off the engine. "Let's watch!" she said.

They got out of the car and leaned against the hood, watching the beautiful sprays of color and the zooming lights and listening to the popping, zinging, and booming.

"Do you want me to take you back to RSC?" asked Dana. "We might be able to catch the tail end of the fireworks."

"Nah, that's okay," said Christina. "They'll probably be over in a couple more minutes anyway." Her stomach growled. She'd missed not only the fireworks but all the food at the picnic too! She wondered if Grace was cozying up to Mike at this very moment, oohing and aahing as the fireworks burst in the sky above. She put the thought out of her mind.

As they pulled into Christina's driveway, Dana stopped the car and turned to Christina. "You were really great with Jen tonight," she said. "Thanks so much for all your help. I'm sorry you missed out on the party."

"No problem," said Christina, hopping out of the car. "I just hope Jen's okay."

Christina let herself in through the kitchen door. She could hear the TV in the other room.

"That you, honey?" called her mother.

"Yep!" she called back, opening the refrigerator and peering in. Her mom was a health nut. She could come back from the grocery store with five bags of food, and still Christina would find nothing she could eat. Luckily, though, she spotted a tub of hummus and a bag of carrots. There was a box of whole wheat crackers in the cupboard. That would work.

She heard her mom pause the movie she was watching. She came in to join Christina at the table. Her mom's cheeks were pink and her eyes were a little shiny. She must have been crying. Christina guessed it wasn't because of the movie. "Did you have fun at the picnic?" her mom asked.

Christina told her about Jen.

"Oh, what a shame."

"So did Dad call?"

Her mother shook her head. "I thought maybe he'd called you on your cell. He seems to prefer that to the home phone."

Christina pulled out her cell phone and checked it. A couple of texts from Ashley and Lindsay, but no other messages or missed calls. "Nothing from Dad," she said in a flat voice.

Her mother patted her hand. "He may have been on call tonight. He probably had no time."

"He was supposed to let me know about my purple shorts," said Christina, feeling anger well up inside. "I left them at his house and he said he'd check the laundry but *obviously* he forgot." She hated getting her mom upset, and she hated to create another reason for her parents to be mad at each other, but she always seemed to be missing stuff that she'd left at one or the other of their houses.

"Honey, you have a lot of shorts."

"But those are my favorite," said Christina through gritted teeth. But she let it drop. Her life had turned upside down when her parents separated late last fall. Now that the divorce was final, she was usually spending Wednesday nights and weekends at her dad's house across town. And because of all the unanticipated expenses this year, her parents had dropped another bomb on her a few weeks ago: For the first time in almost forever, she wouldn't be spending the summer at sleepaway camp. At this point, Christina was long past holding out a tiny ray of hope that her parents would come to their senses and realize how foolishly they'd acted, but she did really want her purple shorts. Sometimes it looked like the only bright spot this summer was joining RSC.

"Don't forget you'll be seeing your father soon enough," her mother reminded her. "You can get them back then. Also, he says he has plans for the weekend for the two of you."

Christina nodded, then swallowed the big lump that had risen in her throat. She had told Ashley about her parents. Ashley's parents were divorced, so Christina figured she'd understand. And she'd also told Lindsay, because whatever you told Ashley, Lindsay was guaranteed to find out. But she hadn't told anyone else—especially old friends like Grace and Mel. It was just too sad for her to talk about it with friends who remembered what her family had been like years ago.

"Guess I'll get ready for bed," said Christina, standing up and clearing her stuff. The house phone rang and Christina leaped to answer it. The caller ID said it was not her dad—it was Coach Dana.

"Hi, Dana," Christina answered. She couldn't imagine why the coach was calling. After all, she had just said goodbye to her a few minutes ago.

"Hey, Christina, I wanted to let you know that they didn't find a fracture in the X-ray they took of Jen's leg," she said. "It's just a bad sprain. She has to be on crutches for a while, but they said she could start some water rehab fairly soon."

"Oh, that's great!" said Christina.

"Listen, I have a proposal for you," said Dana. "The coaches and I could really use an assistant to help us with the big meet next week—and maybe for the rest of the season. You were so impressive tonight with the way you took charge and helped out with Jen. Would you be interested in becoming the team's manager?"

Christina's jaw dropped. "Um, maybe. What would I have to do?"

"You'd help with equipment, timing, recording results, putting up and taking down flags, that kind of thing. And you'd help keep things on schedule during the meet itself, which can get pretty hectic. You wouldn't have to come to all the practices, although it would be great if you could be there as often as possible. How does that sound?"

"Manager!" said Christina, looking up at her mother. Her mother smiled and nodded. "It sounds like it could be really fun." What a great excuse to spend time with Mike Morris! She was sure she could be useful to the boys' team, too. The idea was definitely appealing. "That sounds awesome!" She tried not to sound as crazy excited as she felt.

"Great," said Dana. "Maybe you should put me on with your mom or dad so I can make sure it's okay with them."

"My dad's, um, not here," said Christina, her voice trembling a tiny bit. "But here's my mom."

She handed the phone to her mom with one hand and gave a thumbs-up sign with the other. "Tell her it's okay!" she whispered to her mom, then danced her way up to her room.

Chapter Four

Grace slept poorly that night and prayed for rain so that Tuesday morning's practice would be canceled. It didn't, and it wasn't. Tuesday dawned bright, sunny, and still very hot.

The team was quiet as the girls assembled on the pool deck, stretching, talking in low voices, and waiting for Coach Dana and Coach Michelle to appear. When they did emerge from the locker room, Coach Dana called the older girls together for a meeting. Coach Michelle went off with the younger girls to stretch and then warm up in the water.

"The good news is, Jen's leg is not broken," said Coach Dana.

The girls let out a collective sigh, and the pall over the

group seemed to lift immediately. Grace felt her heart leap within her chest. It wasn't broken!

"But the bad news is," Coach Dana went on, "she's got to be on crutches for a while anyway. It's a bad sprain and seems to be giving her a lot of pain. She'll need our support as she rehabs."

"Who's going to swim in the relay, Coach?" asked Lisa. "She was our anchor!"

"I have to think about who might replace Jen in her events. Actually, Lisa, I'm thinking about moving you from third spot to anchor in the relay. Your freestyle stroke has improved so much already."

"Yess!!" said Lisa, pumping her fist.

"So with Lisa swimming the free, I'm still debating who's going to swim the fly." She stood up. "It's a complicated meet because we'll be competing against teams from five other clubs. But before we go on, I want to introduce someone to you. The coaches and I have been thinking for a while that we can really use a team manager. And we think we've found the perfect person."

Grace had been sitting in the back of the clump of girls, so she had to sit up tall to see who was coming out of the locker room. Not again . . .

"Christina!" shouted Veronica. "Awesome!"

As the other girls scrambled to their feet and surrounded Christina, Grace slumped back down, too stunned to say anything. A huge reason she'd joined RSC was to get away from Christina, to carve out her own place and her own set of friends. It had been bad enough when she'd discovered Christina had joined the club. And now she was going to be the manager of the swim team? And hang out at the one place where Grace finally felt like she belonged? Why was Christina nosing her way into Grace's new life? It was so not fair.

"So, Grace." Coach Dana was squatting down next to her. "I was thinking you would be good for the third leg of the relay. You're strong and you have a great spring off the block."

"Me?" gasped Grace. "Me, do the *butterfly*?"

As Coach Dana nodded, Grace heard a phone buzz. Dana pulled her phone out and checked the text. Her expression went from hopeful to dejected as she read it, but she quickly recovered, put the phone away again, and turned back to Grace. "We have a week and a half to get you up to speed, literally. I need Veronica to fill in for Jen in the individual medley, and of course she'll also be swimming the first leg of the medley relay, the backstroke, as she usually does."

"But I—"

"Grace," said Coach Dana firmly, her clear blue eyes practically boring a hole through Grace, "you can do this. No buts or reasons why you aren't good enough, okay? You're a member of a team, and the team needs you."

Grace flashed back to the image of poor Jen sprawled out and crying, and horrible guilt whooshed through her all over again. "All right," she said in a tiny voice. "I'll do it for the team."

"Good," said Coach Dana, standing up and clapping her hands to get the team's attention. "All right, girls! Everyone into the water. Let's get started with a two hundred pull-kick-pull-swim."

Grace locked eyes with Christina, who smiled and wiggled her fingers hello at her. Was she taunting Grace? Or was she being genuinely friendly? Grace was too miserable to try to figure it out.

Practice that day was grueling. Afterward Grace relaxed in the shallow end, her knees bent, her arms hooked to the edge, and her head resting on the sun-warmed concrete. She was panting and light-headed. Coach Michelle had taken the rest of the divers to the gym to do some dryland training on the trampoline. But Grace had had to stay behind because Coach Dana wanted her to work on her butterfly stroke. Grace loved working on the trampoline. Sometimes the trainer even put you in a harness and you could jump off a springboard into a cushy landing pit. She sighed. She had missed the chance to train with Coach Michelle, and she had not gotten one bit better or faster at swimming. Not only was she responsible for Jen's injury, she was also going to be responsible for the team bombing the relay, and most likely the whole meet.

"Hey, butterfly girl. What's up?"

Grace shaded her eyes and looked up. Justin was looking down at her and grinning. Mike stood next to him, backlit by the late-morning sun. "Not much," she answered, trying to sound casual. She hoped her eyes weren't completely red-rimmed from her goggles, but she could tell by the way her cheeks hurt that they probably were. Hastily she pulled herself out of the water, grabbed her towel, and wrapped it around herself.

"Tough practice?" asked Justin.

"You could say that. Dana wants me to swim the fly at the meet, and I stink at the fly."

She saw Mike nudge Justin. Justin cleared his throat. "If you need help, I—that is, we—could help you out if you want. We both swim the butterfly. It's just getting the timing right, and working on your start."

Grace barely focused on Justin's words. She was too busy wondering about Mike. Why had he just nudged Justin? Had he asked Justin to suggest this? Was he too nervous to ask her this himself? Mike didn't say a lot. Maybe he was just as shy as she was. Maybe secretly he had a crush on her. She willed herself not to blush. "That sounds great, thanks," she said as casually as she knew how.

"We're almost finished with practice," said Justin. "We're just having a quick meeting. How about if we help you with your stroke? Mike and me, that is."

"Um, sure, that sounds great," said Grace, although inside she was screaming "YESSSSSS! YESSSSSSSSSS! YESSSSSSSSSSSSSSSSSS!"

Coach Paul tooted his whistle.

"Gotta go!" said Justin, and he and Mike went over to join the boy swimmers clustered around their coach.

"He's cute," said Christina, who seemed to have appeared at Grace's side out of nowhere. She gestured with her chin in the general direction of the boys' team.

"Who? *Justin?*"

Christina giggled. "Um, no. Not Justin. Coach Paul."

Grace had been lost in thought about what she

was going to say to Mike. She wasn't really focused on Christina. Then Christina's words registered. "You think Coach Paul is cute? He's in *college*," said Grace. "Isn't he a little old for you?"

"I don't mean cute like *our* kind of cute," said Christina, looking horrified. "I mean cute as in cute for Coach Dana."

"Oh! Yeah, I guess so." Grace quickly lost interest. She went back to thinking about her upcoming practice session with Mike. Should she change her bathing suit? Or would that look like she was trying too hard?

"Aw, come on. Don't you think they'd make a nice couple?"

"Who?"

"Dana and Paul!"

"Oh. Yeah, I guess." Grace giggled. "Paul is funny, but Dana is so serious. I have a hard time imagining what they'd talk about together, besides swimming."

"Maybe you're right," said Christina, although she didn't look convinced. Grace knew how stubborn Christina could be. She looked like she was still scheming.

"I guess I'm focusing more on the meet right now. I have to practice my back dive and my reverse dive. They're still kind of messy. And now Dana wants me to swim butterfly in the medley relay."

Christina frowned. "I'm starting to think *you* need to think about something besides swimming too," she said.

"What's that supposed to mean?"

"No offense or anything. But you seem sort of, well, preoccupied with swimming these days."

"I'm just nervous. I'm supposed to swim in the relay and I've never done anything like that before. I'm scared of flubbing my leg of the relay and disqualifying the whole team."

"You'll be fine. Just swim as fast as you can, right? Simple enough."

"Sure," said Grace. *Easy for Christina to say,* she thought. She'd never been interested in competitive sports.

"On the other hand, maybe it's not such a good idea," said Christina.

"What, the relay?"

"No, silly. Getting the coaches together. I can't imagine Dana in a relationship. I mean, have you ever seen her with her hair in anything but a ponytail and wearing anything but gym clothes?"

"That's pretty much all I wear too," said Grace.

"I noticed," said Christina.

Ordinarily Grace would be annoyed by such a comment. But she was focused on practicing her arm movement on the butterfly, which Dana had helped her with in practice, and barely paid any attention to Christina.

"Why are you waving your arms around like that?" asked Christina.

Grace stopped and smiled sheepishly. "Sorry, just working on my stroke. I just realized what Coach Dana showed me today, and I finally get it."

"Okay, whatever. Forget I asked about the coaches," Christina said with a sigh. "But there is one other thing I wanted to talk to you about." Christina looked around to be sure no one was listening. "I was wondering. . . . I see you've been hanging around Mike quite a bit because you guys are both on the swim team. That's one reason why I was so psyched when Coach Dana asked me to be the manager. Would you ask him about me? Like, if he likes me? You know, *like* likes me?"

So *that* was why Christina had agreed to be the manager. She wanted to spend more time with Mike. And now she wanted Grace to talk to him about her? Grace avoided Christina's eyes. She hadn't confessed her crush on Mike to Christina, but that didn't mean she felt like she should help Christina get the guy. "I think he's pretty shy," she said. "He might think it's totally weird if I asked him that. I mean, I don't really hang out with him a lot."

Christina's face crumpled.

Was she about to cry? Inward groan. Grace could not deal with this now. "But I'll try, okay? I'll see if I have a chance to bring it up," said Grace. "He and I have a—well, we're going to hang out after his practice today."

Now Christina looked mad. "Well, for someone who doesn't hang out with Mike much, you're sure spending a lot of time together," she said. "Hope you guys have a great time today." She spun around and walked away.

"So the aim here is to make sure your thumbs go in first. You move your arms in an S shape, like this." Justin and Grace were standing in the pool, and Justin demonstrated the arm movement for her.

Grace watched closely and listened intently. What Justin was saying really made sense. Out of the corner of her eye she watched Mike push off and glide like a seal underwater, then emerge in a sudden burst, attacking the water with his powerful shoulders. She so wished she could do that.

"Um, does that make sense?" Justin asked.

She snapped back to focus on Justin. "Yeah, actually, it does. It helps a lot."

"So it's important to have two kicks for every one rotation of your arms. The kick comes from the hips, and *not* from the knees down. I think that's part of your problem."

Grace nodded. Don't stare at Mike, she told herself fiercely. Not that it was easy to do without Justin noticing. Mike had been "demonstrating" in the pool this whole time. He hadn't really "helped" her one bit. Justin had done all the helping. She sighed. Boys could be so clueless.

Chapter Five

"What's this video you want me to watch again?" asked Christina.

"I'll show you," said Lindsay, pulling Ashley's tablet computer off Ashley's lap. She flopped onto her stomach and quickly typed in the address. "See what I mean?" she said. The three girls shimmied together side by side on Christina's bed and watched a woman in the video sashay out of the surf.

"You put leave-in conditioner in your hair," said Ashley, "and then you pull it back into a ponytail so it stays in place, and use double-stick tape so your bathing suit doesn't ride up when you get out of the water."

"And you use waterproof mascara, and Vaseline on

your eyebrows," Lindsay chimed in, studying the video intently as though she were trying to commit the sequence to memory.

"It sure seems like a lot of effort," said Christina. "I mean, no one looks good dripping wet."

"*She* does," said Ashley, pointing at the woman on the screen.

Lindsay sighed. "One more week and I'll be at the beach. I can't wait to be out of this boring old town."

"I wonder if this technique works getting out of a pool as well as it does for getting out of the ocean?" said Ashley.

"I thought your dad had a place at the beach?" asked Lindsay.

"He does, but there's also a swim club, sort of like RSC, near his beach house," said Ashley. "I shopped for my beach suits and my pool suits—it's really a totally different look, you know."

Christina stifled a yawn, but she managed to turn away so they wouldn't notice. She liked fashion as much as the next person, but Lindsay and Ashley took it extremely seriously. It got a little tedious listening to them talk about nothing but fashion and gossip all the time. On the other hand, with Grace so full of herself these days, well, it was nice to feel like a part of this new group of friends. She got annoyed all over again as she remembered how unenthusiastic Grace had been about her scheme to get the coaches together.

The woman in the video strutted haughtily along the sand and flipped her long ponytail out of the way, oblivious to the admiring glances from all the handsome guys walking by. The whole thing looked ridiculous to Christina. No one looked like that, and no beach she knew had that many good-looking guys walking past. Besides, Mike Morris seemed like the sort of guy who would be more interested in friendly girls, girls who were actually interested in talking about stuff. Girls such as herself.

"How's your swim-manager job thingummy going?" asked Ashley, rolling onto her back and pulling out her phone to text someone. Christina had noticed that Ashley often asked a question and then acted like she wasn't the least bit interested in the answer. Now was one of those times.

"Well, I've only been to two practices, but so far so good," said Christina. "I like that they emphasize fun and team spirit more than winning. Some of the swimmers are pretty hard-core; they swim for their school teams during the school year. But a lot of others don't take it all that seriously and they're pretty fun to hang out with."

"See much of Mike?" asked Lindsay with a sly grin. Even Ashley stopped texting and rolled onto one elbow to hear Christina's response.

Christina had risen to a sitting position, but now she fell backward onto the bed with a huge sigh. "Hot as ever," she said. "But he barely talks to me. I can't decide if he's secretly pining for me and is just painfully shy, or if he hasn't *noticed* how much I am *flirting* with him. Boys can be really clueless."

Lindsay slid off the bed and went over to sit at Christina's desk, which was really more of a vanity table now that it was summer. She peered at herself in the huge round mirror and then picked up a tube of Christina's lip gloss and dabbed a bit on her lips. "You don't think it's because he's just not that into you, do you?" she asked casually, making kissy faces at herself in the mirror.

Christina tried not to look hurt. "Could be, I guess," she said. "But I think it's because he hasn't picked up on things. My new scheme is to figure out a way to set up the girls' coach and the boys' coach. If I can get Mike to help me, it could be a great way for us to spend some 'quality time' together." She crooked her fingers to indicate air quotes.

"How are you planning to get *that* to happen?" asked

Ashley, scrunching her nose as though the whole idea was distasteful to her.

"Well, first I have to find out if Paul has a girlfriend. I asked Mike to let me know, but who knows if he'll actually find out. Then I have to get Dana to see that there's more to life than just swimming."

"What if Dana has a boyfriend?" asked Lindsay.

"I highly doubt Dana has a boyfriend. We'd know if she did."

"Okay, so then what?" prompted Ashley.

"Well. Then I have to come up with some sort of plan to get them together."

"A plan?"

"I need to get Dana into some sort of a predicament. Then Paul can rescue her. I thought of fixing it so her car could run out of gas, but I have no idea how to make a car run out of gas."

"That might be tough," said Lindsay, curling a strand of her long hair around her finger and looking at the ceiling.

"Or I could borrow Coach Michelle's baby and have Paul be playing with him just when Dana is passing by and she'll see them together and think it's so cute that he's taking care of a baby that—"

"That could be seen as kidnapping. Which is a felony,"

Ashley pointed out. "I should know. My dad's a criminal lawyer."

Christina grew quiet. They weren't interested in helping her figure this out, obviously. They seemed much more interested in themselves.

Christina's mom came to the door and knocked lightly before peeking her head inside. "Your father just called," she said to Christina in a flat voice. "He'd like to pick you up in the early afternoon on Friday, rather than dinnertime. I guess he has some outing planned for the two of you."

Christina groaned. "I was going to spend the day at the pool," she said. "He's probably going to drag me somewhere educational again, like he did last weekend. I don't think I can stand another planetarium show while the rest of the world is lounging poolside."

Her mother didn't say anything but shrugged a tiny bit. "You can call him to discuss it if you like," she said, her voice wobbling ever so slightly. She closed the door behind her.

Ashley stopped texting and gave Christina a sympathetic look. "It's hard at first, I know. You'll get used to it, though. When my parents first split up I had to be the one to pass messages back and forth, since they weren't even speaking to each other. And I felt like I never had the clothes I needed, the schoolbooks I needed, all that stuff. No matter which place I was in, I realized my stuff was at the other one."

Christina nodded. That was just what she had been experiencing too, but she didn't dare say anything for fear she might cry.

The three girls were silent for a few minutes. Suddenly the phone in Ashley's hand started playing her ringtone. Ashley looked at the caller name. Her face lit up and she answered it. She mouthed the name Nick to the other girls.

Christina was relieved to have the focus shift away from her parents' divorce. As she listened to Ashley giggle into her phone, an idea struck her like a thunderclap.

"What?" asked Lindsay, who'd seen Christina's face reflected in the vanity mirror.

"I just figured out the perfect way to get them together!"

Ashley finished her conversation with Nick. "Who?"

"The coaches!"

Lindsay swiveled around in her chair. "How?"

"I'll steal Dana's phone."

"You'll what?" both girls said at the same time.

"I mean, I won't *really* steal it. I'll just temporarily take it when she's not watching, and then I'll plant it somewhere where Paul will be sure to find it. She'll be looking all over for it and then he'll swoop in with it and hand it over to her to save the day. They'll look into each other's eyes, and . . . the rest will be history!"

There was a moment's silence. Then Lindsay spoke. "That. Is. Awesome."

"Perfect!" said Ashley.

"And maybe I can get Mike to help me with the plan, and then he and I can both get credit, and maybe we'll even get asked to make a toast at the wedding and . . . and . . ." She trailed off, giddy with excitement.

"It makes me wish I could be a member at RSC," said Ashley wistfully.

"Me too!" said Lindsay. "There's so much excitement there."

"Well, you guys aren't exactly going to be hurting for excitement this summer," Christina said. "You're both about to head off to your families' fabulous summer beach houses."

"Still. You have to let us know if it works out," said Ashley.

"Don't worry. I'll text you guys and let you know what develops."

Chapter Six

Grace practiced intensely for the next two days, still feeling heavy with guilt. The heat wave continued, with the temperature well into the nineties every day. Everyone on the swim team seemed to feel Jen's absence, but Grace was sure she felt it most of all. She would never be able to swim half as well as Jen, but she felt like she had to try her absolute hardest. Most of the other girls just swam for fun and didn't take the competitions very seriously. Why did such a thing have to happen to Jen?

On Thursday, Grace finally got to practice some diving, after two days of only swimming. She had her dive sheet for the meet next week all written out. She'd chosen six dives that she felt pretty good about. The degree of difficulty wasn't all that high, especially for the first few, but at least she wouldn't embarrass herself or the team.

"Try the reverse one-and-a-half tuck," said Coach Michelle as Grace emerged from the water after a dive. "Remember, I want a nice, tight tuck this time."

Grace gulped as she walked up the diving board ladder. This was her hardest dive. It had a 2.1 degree of difficulty. Uh-oh. Out of the corner of her eye she saw Mike, Justin, and Kyle Lundgren amble over and sit down. Were they going to watch her? Her heart bounced up to her throat.

"Concentrate, Grace," said Coach Michelle, as though she could read Grace's thoughts.

Grace tried to put everything out of her mind except the dive. Not easy with all that was going on these days. She knew she needed to get high on the takeoff. Taking four quick steps for her approach, she drove her knee up and bounced high into the air, throwing herself backward and tucking her legs tightly to her chest as she rotated. She kicked out strong and extended her arms toward the water, but the front of her legs slammed—ow!—the surface of the water.

"You're getting there," said Coach Michelle as Grace's head popped up from the water and she pulled herself out of the pool. Grace fought every urge to look over to where

Mike had been sitting. She was way too embarrassed by her dive. "But you overrotated," Michelle continued. "You need to come out of your tuck sooner, and make sure your arms are by your ears. They were too far in front of you."

After practice, as Grace stood toweling off near the pool, she heard Veronica shrieking with excitement. Jen was back! Kind of.

Grace hurried over to see her along with the rest of the team. Jen, wearing a bathing suit and shorts, was leaning on her crutches and laughing and chatting with the team. Grace couldn't meet her eye.

"They're letting me start rehab today!" she said. "I get to unstrap this brace and get into the water finally!"

Coach Dana clapped her hands to get the girls' attention. "All right, everyone, time to head out and leave Jen to the pool. She has a lot of work to do. Grace, stick around."

Grace felt her breath leave her. Had Dana found out that she, Grace, was responsible for what had happened to Jen? Was she going to accuse her in front of Jen? Grace would have to leave RSC forever. She could never show her face here again. She'd have to spend the rest of the summer hiding under her bed.

"Uh, Grace? Join us on planet earth?" said Dana with a half smile. "I was going to suggest that you and Jen have a little powwow about the relay. I think a lot of what's bothering you is in your head. So much about swimming well is focus and mind-set, right, Jen?"

Jen nodded, then turned and smiled at Grace. "Yeah, that and having a good start!" she said with a laugh. "Come on, Grace. You can keep me company while I do my leg lifts," she said, hobbling to the edge of the pool.

Numbly, Grace followed her. Jen clomped over to the stairs, laid her crutches down, and stripped down to her bathing suit. "I'm allowed to walk in the water and do leg lifts," she said, lowering herself in and wincing a little as she touched the bottom. "And pretty soon they'll let me tread water, and then do some gentle flutter kicks," she added.

Say something, Grace told herself firmly. *I must have guilt written all over my face.* She cleared her throat. "So does it hurt a lot?" she asked a bit too brightly.

"Not much. Well, a little," admitted Jen. She was leaning back on the stairs, gently kicking her legs under the water. Grace noticed she kept flinching a little bit, as though something hurt. "The physical therapist says I can do gentle stuff in the water but not to put any weight on it out of the water. It just feels so good to be in the pool again. It doesn't feel like summer if I'm not in the pool." She smiled at Grace.

This just made Grace feel worse. It would make things

so much easier if Jen were mean or stuck-up. But she was so sweet.

"So anything I can help you with for the relay?" Jen asked.

"Oh, well, um, I guess the idea is to swim as fast as I can, right?" said Grace with a forced little laugh.

"Actually, the key is to relax," said Jen. "I know that's easy to say when you're not all nervous and trying to make up time, but really it's the best way to improve your speed. And also getting a good start."

"Jen, how does it feel?" said Coach Dana, walking over to the girls. She was standing at the side of the pool, her arms crossed and her brow furrowed.

"Great!" said Jen.

Coach Dana frowned. "That's probably enough for today," she said. "I'd like to have a talk with your mom when she comes to pick you up."

Jen darted a glance at Grace and rolled her eyes, but she obediently moved toward the stairs and allowed Coach Dana to help her out and hand her the crutches. "Remember," she said to Grace, "relax and do a lot of stretching!"

For quite some time after everyone else had left, Grace sat by herself at the side of the pool, swishing her legs in the water. An adult swim came and went, but Grace didn't feel like getting back in the pool. There weren't many recreational swimmers at RSC today, probably because the sky was overcast. She loved the way the water rolled and bubbles roiled when she made little upward pushes with her feet, and the sound of the gently lapping water soothed her frayed nerves a bit. She sat lost in thought about Jen.

"Hi, Grace."

She turned. Justin. Not exactly who she felt like chatting with right now. In fact, she didn't feel like chatting with anyone. "Hi," she said. "Thanks again for helping me out the other day."

"You're welcome."

They both listened to the lapping water.

"So I was just wondering something," Justin said at last. "You know that new movie *Man vs. Ant*? About ants living in a nuclear power plant that become the size of cars and then march into the city and even the Special Forces' tanks can't penetrate their exoskeletons?"

"I guess so."

"Well, guess what? It just opened at the theater down the block from here!"

"Oh. Uh-huh."

"So, a few of us are going this afternoon? And I thought maybe you might like to come too?"

"Who, me? Oh. No, sorry, I can't," said Grace. All she wanted to do was go home and do some painting in the quiet of her own room. Besides, who wanted to see a movie about giant, man-eating ants? "I, um, I have to go home and clean my room or my mom is going to kill me."

Justin's face fell. "Okay, cool," he said with a little shrug. "I'll let you know how it is."

"Thanks, yeah, I can't wait to hear," said Grace. She barely waved as he turned and walked off, scuffing his flip-flops in the wet parts of the pool deck.

She sighed and pulled her feet out of the water. As she was about to stand up and head into the locker room, she heard someone talking behind her. It was Coach Paul, leaning against the snack-bar building, his back to Grace, having a hushed conversation over the phone.

"But what difference does that make if we want to make it work?" Paul asked.

Silence while he listened.

"I know. I understand. But—"

Another long pause while the person on the other end said something else.

"I just think if it's really special, it has to work. And what we had *was* really special, and—"

Another silence as he listened.

"They have no idea."

Listening.

"All right. I don't get it, but I guess I have to deal. You're probably right. . . . You too. I hope we can keep things normal moving forward. I'll try, too."

Grace knew she shouldn't be eavesdropping. But she was transfixed. Coach Paul was usually so cool, so seemingly in control and confident. Now he clicked off his phone, heaved a deep sigh, and sank down into a crouch, his head on his folded arms. He sat for a minute like that, then slowly stood back up. He looked dejected. Sighing deeply, he trudged away.

So. Paul and his girlfriend appeared to have just broken up, or so it seemed to Grace. Her first thought was to text Christina. Hadn't she mentioned something about wanting to know if Paul had a girlfriend? Well, now he didn't, but Grace wasn't going to talk about it with Christina. That was out of the question. Not with the way Christina was acting these days. And besides, the only reason she cared about getting the coaches together was because she thought it would help her get closer to Mike. No way was Grace going to bother with it.

In the locker room she ran into Jaci, who was braiding her wet hair.

"So, you going to the movie with us?" Jaci demanded.

"What movie? Oh. The giant *ant* movie? No," Grace said with a chuckle. "I passed on that."

Jaci put down her hairbrush and eyed Grace in the mirror. "Do not tell me you blew off Justin McGee. He's been trying to get up the courage to ask you out for, like, weeks."

Grace's jaw dropped. "Are we talking about *Justin* Justin? Justin-on-the-swim-team Justin?"

"Yep. You are so dense sometimes, Grace Davis," said Jaci with a wry smile.

"So that was a kind of, sort of ask-out?"

"No kind of, sort of about it. He asked you out, and you apparently iced him."

It took a moment for Grace's brain to process this information. How *could* she have been so dense? For the first time ever in her whole life, she'd gotten asked out! And she'd been so preoccupied by the meet, and by what she'd done to Jen, that she hadn't even registered that that was what had happened!

She sat down heavily on a bench. Did she even like Justin like that? She just hadn't ever considered him in that light.

"Did you know he has an identical twin?" asked Jaci.

"He *does*?"

"Yep. But Jasper, his twin, is the complete opposite of Justin. Justin's the jock half, all about sports. I hear Justin is smart but an underachiever. But Jasper! I met him at an interdistrict math competition. He's in honor society, plays bassoon, hates sports, and is really loud and outspoken. In short, the perfect man." Jaci stuffed her brush into her bag. "I'll let you know how the movie is," she said over her shoulder. "Hey, I can think of worse movies to go to than one about man-eating arthropods."

Chapter Seven

It finally rained over the weekend, and the suffocating heat lifted a bit at last. Monday morning there wasn't a cloud in the sky, but the weatherman promised the temperature would stay below eighty. Christina hadn't forgotten about her plan for the coaches, but the opportunity just hadn't presented itself. Then during practice, she finally got her chance.

She'd been over at the diving area transferring everyone's diving sheets onto the main list for Friday's meet, and wondering how to get Mike to pay attention to her, when Coach Michelle called her over.

"Can you go ask Coach Dana to come over here if she has a second? I want her to have a look at Grace's form on the inward dive and give me a second opinion."

"Sure," said Christina. "I think she's free right now—everyone's busy swimming their ten-by-fifties, so she's just hanging out." Christina took the long way, around the other pool, on her way to find Coach Dana, so she could catch a glimpse of Mike. She spotted him as he was pulling himself out of the pool, every muscle in his back glinting in the morning sun. *He certainly didn't need Vaseline or double-stick tape to look hot coming out of the water,* she thought.

She found Coach Dana stacking kickboards. Was it her imagination, or did Dana look really upset? She decided she was imagining it and delivered Coach Michelle's message. "I can finish up here," said Christina, taking the stack of kickboards out of Dana's arms.

"Thanks, Christina. You're a big help," said Coach Dana. She smiled at Christina, but her eyes looked sad. *All the more reason she needs someone to cheer her up,* Christina thought. Christina still didn't know if Paul had a girlfriend, but she was through with waiting.

As soon as Christina thought the coast was clear, she headed over to the table where Coach Dana had left her bag. Setting a large stack of kickboards alongside the bag, she pretended to straighten out the pile. With her other hand, she reached into Dana's bag, and almost immediately her hand closed around the phone. Darting a quick glance around to be sure no one saw her, Christina slipped the phone out of Dana's bag and into the front pocket of her shorts.

When Dana returned ten minutes later, Christina had stacked all the kickboards neatly in their area. "Be right back. Coach Paul needs a couple extra pull buoys," she said to Dana, and headed toward the boys' lanes.

Dana furrowed her brow. "Really? That's funny. He was just telling me the other day that he doesn't use them much because they inhibit core rotation."

"Oh, I know *that*," Christina said, as though it were the most obvious statement in the world. "He uses them for, um, something completely different, but . . . it's still in the experimental phase," she finished lamely.

Dana just shrugged and returned to the swimmers.

As Christina neared the lanes where the boys were practicing, it suddenly struck her: How would she ever find Coach Paul's stuff? One of the tables had a bunch of backpacks and towels on it and several pairs of flip-flops underneath. Then a younger boy walked past her. Thinking fast, she grabbed a clean RSC pool towel from a nearby stack and stopped him. "Can you tell me which bag belongs to

Coach Paul?" she asked the kid. "He wants me to leave this towel for him."

The kid pointed to a black backpack propped on a chair next to the table of stuff. "That one," he said.

Christina thanked him and sidled up to the table. Quickly she tilted the bag and shoved Dana's phone behind it. Paul would surely find the phone first and come to Dana's rescue when she couldn't find it. No one seemed to have noticed. She kept walking and didn't even scan the swimmers in the water to see which one was Mike.

After practice ended, Coach Dana and Coach Michelle assembled the older girls in the seating area for a conference. "I have some disappointing news," said Coach Dana. "It turns out that Jen's leg is not just sprained. It was giving her a lot of pain so her parents took her in for another X-ray, and unfortunately this time the doctors found a fracture. So she'll probably be out of competition for the rest of the summer."

All the girls groaned. Christina noticed that Grace looked especially stricken. The blood seemed to drain from her face and she looked like she might throw up. *I didn't think Grace and Jen were especially close, so why is Grace taking this so hard*? she wondered.

Coach Dana was fumbling in her bag. "Hey, where's

my phone?" she said. Several girls came over to help her look under towels, beneath chairs, and inside nearby bags. Dana's searching became more urgent. "It was here, I know it was here," she muttered, taking out the entire contents of her bag and putting them down on the table one by one.

Christina felt giddy with nervous anticipation. The plan was working! She hadn't expected Dana to be quite so upset, though. And where was Coach Paul? She realized she hadn't conceived a plan to get him over here from the boys' side of the pool. He was talking to a couple of boys near the starting blocks and was completely clueless about the drama that was playing out nearby. She had to do something. "I'll go see if Coach Paul knows where it is!" she said.

Coach Dana gave her a baffled look, as if to say, Why would *he* know where it is? But she was clearly too distracted to give it more thought and resumed searching. Veronica and several other girls from the team helped her.

"Um, excuse me, Coach Paul," said Christina, who had stood by respectfully, waiting for a pause in his conversation with the swim-team boys. "Coach Dana can't find her cell phone. Have you seen it anywhere?"

Coach Paul looked at Christina, slightly bewildered. "No, I—why would I . . . Did she ask you to ask me that?"

"Kind of."

He looked at her, still baffled. "No, sorry, I haven't seen it," he said.

"Maybe somehow it got mixed up with some towels over here or something," suggested Christina, although she knew that sounded lame.

Paul looked over at Dana, who was now on her hands and knees, searching through the foliage in a potted plant. "Come on, guys, let's see if we can help her find it," he said, and they all headed over to where the girls were searching.

"I don't know what could have happened," said Dana, who, to Christina's horror, looked like she might cry. "I never lose stuff. And with my grandmother sick and all, this is really bad that I can't be reached, and . . ."

"How about if I call it?" suggested Paul, reaching into his shorts pocket and pulling out his cell phone. "Is the ringer on?"

Dana nodded, teary-eyed, and Paul pulled up her number. Christina had a creeping feeling that her seemingly foolproof plan was a little less than foolproof. But she felt powerless to do anything.

"Shhh!" Veronica said to the other kids. "Let's listen and see if we hear it!"

"Oh, I don't think calling it is going to work!" said Christina, rushing over to say something, anything, to drown out the ringtones that would expose where the phone actually was. "Because, see, what if it's actually on vibrate and, um—"

"Hey! Hush up, wouldja?" Paul said sharply to her.

She hushed. She swallowed hard. In the sudden silence around the pool, they could all hear the lapping of the water, and also, a quarter of the way around the pool, where all the boys' stuff was heaped, a tinny but distinguishable salsa ringtone.

"That's my phone!" yelled Dana, hurrying toward the sound. A clump of kids and Coach Paul followed after her. Christina dragged her feet at the back of the pack. She watched Dana pounce triumphantly on Paul's black backpack, pick it up, and brandish the ringing phone, which had been stuck behind it. "It's here!" she said delightedly. Then her face clouded over. "Why is it here? What's it doing near this backpack?"

"Hey, Coach!" said Mike. "Isn't that *your* backpack?"

"Well, huh. As a matter of fact, it *is* my backpack," said Paul, looking extremely confused.

"And you have no idea how my phone happened to be under it?" Dana demanded.

"No. I have no idea how your phone ended up here."

"You don't." This was spoken not as a question but as a

dripping-with-sarcasm statement. Dana's tone said "I don't believe one word of what you are saying to me."

Paul clearly understood Dana's tone. "No," he said with some heat. "I really don't. Are you implying I *took* your phone?"

"Well, it didn't just walk over here," she spat back. "I know you're all into practical jokes with your boys, but this? This is not funny." Her blue eyes blazed. "Especially after . . ." She stopped and pressed her lips together.

The rest of the kids were looking from Paul to Dana and back to Paul as they spoke, as though they were watching a Ping-Pong game. Christina just stood wringing her hands.

"If this is the thanks I get for just trying to be helpful, well . . . you're *welcome*!" said Paul.

Almost at the same time, Dana and Paul seemed to realize that they were having an argument in front of both teams.

Dana turned on her heel, muttering something to the girls about being on time tomorrow. Paul just stood there, his mouth open, as though he hadn't quite processed what had just happened. The kids all moved away, breaking into small, murmuring groups. Christina clapped a hand to her forehead and dragged it down the side of her face. "Oh no," she moaned under her breath.

Chapter Eight

The day after the coaches' big fight, Grace sat panting at the edge of the pool. She'd just finished a series of sprints, and now her whole body ached. Her head felt like it was stuffed with cotton, and her lungs burned. She was convinced beyond all doubt that her team was going to lose the relay and that it would all be totally and completely her fault. Veronica would be starting out with backstroke, then Nandini Pratterji for breaststroke, then Grace with butterfly, then Lisa for freestyle. Why did she have to get chosen for butterfly, of all the strokes? It was far and away the hardest one.

She lifted her goggles and snapped them in place on top of her cap. She watched the rest of the girls getting out of the water, toweling off, and chatting and laughing and acting like the whole thing was fun. It was so not fun. *Why do I care so much?* she asked herself. She knew the answer: Because Jen would care. Because Jen was the one swimmer on the team for whom swimming meant everything. And Grace had caused her accident. She owed it to Jen to do well on Friday. What if someone put two and two together and realized she was to blame for Jen's leg? What if Mike or Justin suddenly remembered the sunblock she'd poured onto the pool deck? And even if they didn't, what if Justin never spoke to her again after she'd blown off that movie he'd invited her to?

Justin. Maybe she could make it up to him. Maybe she could get him to help her just a little more. What he'd said last week had been so helpful. He really knew what he was doing and he seemed like a born teacher.

"Hi, Justin," said Grace. Her heart was thumping so hard she wondered if people could hear it.

"Hi," muttered Justin, barely looking up at her. He and Mike and another boy—was his name Tom or Kyle?—were sitting at a table at the snack bar, eating mounds of food. It must have been a tough practice, Grace figured.

"Is Marty having a half-price sale on egg-and-cheese sandwiches or something?" Grace joked.

Mike looked at her blankly. "No, they were the regular price. We're just hungry," he said.

Fail. *Mike never seems to think anything I say is funny,* Grace thought. She was beginning to think that was him, though, not her. Could it be possible that Mike didn't have a sense of humor?

"How was the movie?" she asked, turning to Justin.

Justin blushed. "The movie? Oh. It was pretty good, I guess."

Mike nudged Justin and rolled his eyes. "Pretty good? You've been talking about it nonstop since Thursday!"

Justin grinned, ducked his head, and looked squarely at Grace. "Okay, it was totally awesome."

Grace giggled. Really, he was kind of cute, in an ears-sticking-out kind of way. Not Mike-caliber, of course. Mike was still in a category of hotness all by himself. But if she was totally honest with herself, she found herself thinking about Justin more these days, and not Mike.

"So there's, like, this huge storm? And these giant ants? They almost get washed away? But then they figure out how to form, like, a giant ant clump? And they roll around in the water so no ant is ever stuck underwater for long and that's how they survive drowning? And then—"

The other boy groaned, and Mike put up a hand close to Justin's face in a halt position. "Okay, okay, she gets it," he said. "Spare us, would you? We've heard it all. Maybe you can sit here and tell Grace all about it and we'll make ourselves scarce." He and the other kid stood up, cleared away their stuff, and left Justin and Grace alone.

Don't go! Grace thought, out of habit, as she watched Mike walk away. Did he think she was boring? Maybe she shouldn't have asked Justin about the movie. But she had to see if Justin was still mad at her, because she needed a favor . . .

There was a second of awkward silence. Grace could feel her ears getting hot. She ignored this predictable reaction, and spoke. "Sorry I couldn't go to the movie with you. It sounds awesome."

Justin shrugged. "It was pretty good. Not great."

"It sounded pretty exciting the way you talked about it."

He smiled broadly. "Actually, yeah, it was really exciting. I like horror movies. And bugs. And horror movies about bugs."

Grace took a deep breath. "So I was wondering. . . . Remember how I have to swim in the medley relay on Friday? I'm still really nervous about it. I've never done a relay before, and I'm so scared I'm going to disqualify my team, because, well, I don't really know how to time my start and stuff. You're in the relay, aren't you?"

Justin nodded. "I know a couple of easy tips I could show you that could help you not be so nervous," he said.

"Do you, that is, would you mind showing me some stuff right now?"

He grinned wider than ever.

She'd never noticed the sprinkle of freckles across his nose or what a nice smile he had. And it was so much easier to talk to Justin than to try to think up something to talk about with Mike.

"Come on. Let's go to the other lap pool, and I'll show you how to explode off the block. You're already a good diver so your start should be pretty strong."

She followed after him happily. They passed Mike and Christina, who were having a serious-looking conversation.

"You guys heading to the other pool?" Mike called to them.

"We're practicing starts. You want to come?" Justin called back.

Mike said something quickly to Christina and hurried to catch up with Grace and Justin. Christina flashed an angry look at Grace and walked away.

Ahh! Grace thought. *Maybe Mike really does secretly like me! He just ditched Christina to come be with us!* She couldn't help but be pretty excited to spend the afternoon with two guys she liked.

"Too bad the coaches had that big fight, huh?" said Justin as the three of them stood together next to the water.

"Yeah," agreed Grace. "That was so weird about the phone. Do you think Paul really took it as a practical joke?"

Mike shook his head. "Don't think so."

"I don't think he did it, either," said Justin. "He has a better sense of humor than that."

"Maybe some kid took it," said Grace.

"But why would someone risk getting caught rummaging through Dana's stuff?" asked Justin. "That's a good way to get kicked off the team for good."

A thought struck Grace. Could it have been Christina and her dumb plan to get the two coaches together? She dismissed the idea immediately. Christina was a flirt and could act like a total bubblehead, but playing practical jokes wasn't her style. She was too obsessed with the latest fashions and gossiping about guys. "It's just so awful that two of our coaches aren't speaking to each other," said Grace. "At the beginning of the season they seemed to really get along. I always saw them sitting together, comparing notes.

Then they kind of stopped doing that. And now they won't even *speak* to each other. Coach Dana keeps asking Coach Michelle to deliver messages to Coach Paul. Or she sends Christina. It's too bad, actually, because I like them both so much." Grace tried to give them her best coy smile. "It's almost like they got into a lovers' quarrel."

Oops. Maybe that was the wrong thing to say. Both boys looked uncomfortable. She was still not used to flirting—and last time she'd tried it had obviously ended in disaster with Jen's fall. She made a mental note not to talk too much about other people's relationships or use words like "love." It clearly made boys nervous. "Okay, so can you show me that technique you were talking about with the start?" she said quickly.

Justin went over to the side of the pool deck and grabbed a flotation noodle.

Jordan the lifeguard gave him a "what's up?" gesture from up on his chair.

"Just borrowing it for practicing starts!" Justin called up to him.

Jordan gave him a thumbs-up sign and went back to twirling his whistle lanyard and scoping the pool.

"Okay, so, first, you need a little extra distance on your dive, I noticed," he said. "To get more distance you need to get your hips up higher and change the angle as you come off the block. You can practice diving over this thing. It'll force you to dive out and over it, rather than straight in."

Grace nodded as she took her position on the block, listening carefully.

Justin crouched next to the starting block and held the noodle up across Grace's lane, slightly above the surface of the water. "What's important to remember is that your timing is everything in a relay start. Remember, you can start your dive and be completely stretched out over the water as long as your toes are still on the block when the incoming swimmer touches the wall. Mike, you be the incoming swimmer, okay? I'll hold the noodle like this and, Grace, you dive over it. But be sure to watch him coming in and don't leave too early or you'll be disqualified."

For the next half hour the three of them practiced, taking turns being the diver, the incoming swimmer, and the one holding the noodle.

"I really feel like I'm getting it now!" Grace said excitedly, just after her head had popped out of the water from her dive.

"Good, because now you have to work on finishing," said Justin. "You're the third leg in the relay, remember, so it's important to stick the wall. Don't let up during the last five yards, because your teammate—Lisa, is it?—is going to be timing her start based on how you finish."

Grace nodded, concentrating hard. There was so much to learn, and the meet was now just three days away. But it was all starting to make sense. They spent another fifteen minutes working on the finish.

"Okay, your turn to help me," said Justin. "Can you tell me what I'm doing wrong with my front one-and-a-half dive? Something's not right."

They moved over to the diving area, where Grace and Mike set up chairs alongside the one-meter springboard and critiqued Justin's technique.

Justin first attempted an inward somersault and landed flat on his face.

Grace and Mike managed to stop laughing before Justin's head emerged from the water.

"YOW!" he yelled.

"You're almost there," Grace called to him. "You need to be tighter on your tuck and come out sooner."

"Easy for you to say," he grumbled. "Not all of us are born ballerinas."

"I was a gymnast, not a ballerina," Grace corrected him with a grin. "Now, try it again!" *It feels good to be a little like an expert at something,* she thought proudly.

Gradually, it was starting to dawn on her that maybe, just maybe, she might like Justin as much as Mike. Justin was so good-natured and fun to tease! It also was fun to be sitting next to Mike, and as long as they kept the topic on swimming or diving, she felt comfortable with him. She thought about taking Mike aside at one point and asking what he thought about Christina, as Christina had asked her to do. But the timing just didn't feel right. Mike wasn't the kind of guy with whom you could easily bring up something like that. She didn't want to spoil this moment the three of them were having together.

Chapter Nine

Christina watched Grace walk up to the table where Mike and Justin were sitting with Kyle Lundgren. Grace had been shy as long as Christina had known her, but these days she seemed to need to be right in the middle of the action at all times. It had always been she, Christina, who had been the bold one, the one not afraid to go right up to a group of people and talk to them. What had happened to Grace? What had made her change so quickly?

She wondered if Grace had said anything to Mike about her yet. Did Grace like him too? She watched Grace chatting away with the three boys, and then Mike and Kyle stood up and left the table, so Grace and Justin were sitting by themselves. She didn't know Justin—he lived in the next town over and went to Central Middle School—but he didn't seem like the boyfriend type. Hmm, could it be possible that Grace liked him? No way. Grace was taller than he was. She was startled out of her musings when she noticed Mike coming over to talk to her.

"What's up?" he greeted as he approached her.

"Not much," she said. "Just helping Coach Dana and Coach Michelle figure out the order of events and stuff. It's more complicated than I thought. If someone's both a swimmer and a diver, I don't want to put her events too close together or she could miss her turn or she could be really tired from having just competed." Was he even listening to her? His eyes were scanning the pool behind her, as though he wasn't paying attention to a word she said.

"So, you coming to the pool party here on Friday night?" he asked casually, still not looking at her.

Wait. Was he asking her to the party? Like, asking her out? He made it so hard to tell! "Uh, I guess so." In fact, she'd been trying on different outfit combinations for a week now. "Are you going?"

"Yeah, but on the later side."

Silence. So he wasn't asking her out. Fail. She was determined to keep the conversation going, though. "I just love dancing, don't you? If it's the right music, of course."

Mike shrugged. "I'm not so good at dancing, actually."

"I don't believe that. You're such a good athlete. You must be able to dance a little."

Mike shook his head. "Not my thing, I guess. Anyway, the reason I asked if you're going is that I signed up to sell raffle tickets from five to six, but I can't make it till later. I'm going to my friend's meet and it's away that day. Do you know anyone who could sub for me?"

"Don't worry about it," she said. "I'll cover for you."

He grinned at her. He had the most beautiful smile. "Thanks. I owe you."

"No big deal."

Her mind was whirling. Maybe this was kind of, sort of, his way of asking her to the party? Maybe he was so awkward, he was making this whole thing up about his friend's meet just to see if she planned to be there? He was so hard to figure out!

"Too bad about the coaches, right?"

She looked at him sharply. "What do you mean?"

"I mean, how they're barely talking to each other. Kind of a problem when they have a big meet to put together in three days."

"Oh, that. Do you really think they're that mad at each other?" She tried to keep the worry out of her voice.

"Yeah, they seem pretty mad. This could be a long rest of the summer."

Christina let out a ragged breath. This was all her fault.

"You guys heading to the other pool?" Mike called to Grace and Justin, who were passing by.

"We're practicing starts. You want to come?" Justin called back.

Mike turned to Christina. "So see you later, I guess," he said. "Thanks for covering for me at the party." He trotted off after them.

Well, that was just great. Grace knew full well that Christina liked Mike, and now she was dragging him away during one of the few conversations Christina and Mike had ever had! She met Grace's gaze and scowled at her. Grace just looked away and kept walking.

Christina was still mad at Grace as she finished working out who was swimming which events and consolidating diving sheets to show who was diving which dives, and delivered them to Dana and Michelle. She looked over at Grace, Mike, and Justin for what seemed like the thousandth time. They'd been doing all kinds of swimming drills. But now the boys had left, and Grace was sitting by herself at the edge of the pool. For some reason, when Christina saw Grace sitting there by herself, she felt a wave of warm memories. After all, they'd been in preschool together! On an impulse, Christina decided to set down the clipboard and go talk to her old friend.

"Hi," she said, slipping off her flip-flops.

"Hi," said Grace. She looked a little surprised to see Christina, but not unhappy about it. Christina sat down next to Grace. They both dangled their feet in the sun-flecked, aqua-blue water.

Neither girl spoke for a while as they sat side by side, kicking their feet, languidly swooshing around the water. Then Christina finally said, "So guess what."

"What?"

"You know how Coach Dana and Coach Paul are so mad at each other?"

"Yeah. It's bad."

"Well, it's all my fault."

"*Your* fault? How come?"

"I took her phone. I stuck it next to his bag."

Grace's eyes widened. "Oh!"

Christina sighed. "Remember that plan I mentioned to you last week? How I was trying to figure out a way for them to like each other? Well, I needed Paul to come to the rescue and save the day and that would make Dana eternally grateful and they'd fall in love and get married and have a whole swim team's worth of babies. But my plan kind of backfired. Instead of being in love, they hate each other."

"Oh," said Grace, who looked as though she was pondering this.

"Are you going to tell on me?"

"No," said Grace quickly. "We all do dumb things. I recently did a dumb thing too."

Christina waited.

"You know how Jen hurt herself? That was . . . that was *my* fault."

Now it was Christina's turn to look shocked. "How could it be your fault? I saw the whole thing. You were nowhere near her when she fell."

Grace told her about the sunblock she'd smeared on the pool deck in order to draw a picture.

Christina whistled softly. "Oh. I guess it really *was* your fault."

"Thanks a lot," said Grace drily.

"I mean, no offense, but you must feel really terrible."

Grace blinked at her. "Yeah, I do. About as terrible as you must feel about making our coaches hate each other."

"Okay, good point." Christina sighed, then sank into her own thoughts. It seemed strange to be talking to Grace like they were strangers, filling each other in on big events of their lives. Along with their friend, Mel Levy, Grace and Christina had always been joined at the hip. Grace should have helped her with this plan. Christina couldn't remember a time, until just recently, when they hadn't told each other all their deepest, darkest secrets. She missed Grace.

Grace seemed lost in thought too. Christina wondered if Grace was thinking about how much she missed her.

"So what made you decide not to go to sleepaway camp?" Grace asked.

"I couldn't. We couldn't afford it. See, my parents split up." Christina just blurted it out. It felt so weird to say the words out loud, and to Grace of all people. On the other hand, Grace had known Christina's parents her whole life.

The words hung in the air between them.

"That's not possible," said Grace. "I mean, I'm so sorry! What happened?"

Christina shrugged. It was a relief to tell someone who knew her parents so well. Grace had practically been a member of their family for a while. "They just decided they didn't want to live together," she said dully.

"Maybe they'll get back together?" ventured Grace. She looked like she had no idea what one should say at a time like this.

"Maybe. But I don't think so."

An ancient couple approached the steps on the far side of the pool. The man held the woman's hand as she carefully made her way down the steps. She had on an old-fashioned bathing cap, with a strap under the chin. He wore billowy swim trunks, cinched tightly at his waist. When the woman was safely in, he followed her into the water. They each took a lane and began swimming, the woman in a modified kind of breaststroke with her head never going below the water, the man in a leisurely crawl. The girls watched them for a moment.

"I love old people who are still in love," said Christina, watching the two swim. Then she turned to Grace. "So what are you going to do about Jen?"

"I don't know. I can't even sleep very well most nights. I just feel so terrible."

"I think you should talk to her. You'll feel better if you just tell her."

"But what if she gets really mad? What if she tells the whole team, and they decide to kick me off?" Her voice had begun to quaver.

Christina pulled one leg out of the water and hugged her knee closely. "I don't think she'll get mad. She's the nicest person ever. Anyway, it wasn't like you did it on purpose. You didn't mean to make her fall."

Grace nodded. "I guess you're right. What are you going to do about the coaches?"

Christina rested her forehead on her knee and sighed. "I don't know."

"I think you should tell them too," said Grace. "Just tell Dana the truth."

"She'll think I'm the worst manager in the world!" wailed Christina. "She'll fire me!"

"She might," admitted Grace. "But you know it's wrong for her to go on blaming Paul for something he didn't do."

Christina nodded. "You're right. So when should we tell people? Should we wait until after the meet on Friday?"

Grace shook her head grimly. "I think we have to tell them before. The coaches have to be on speaking terms and be cooperating with each other during the meet. And I won't swim well until I've cleared the air with Jen. I just know it."

"Okay, then," said Christina, already feeling better. "So we have a pact. I tell the coaches what I did, you tell Jen what you did. Deal?" She held out her hand.

Grace took her hand and gave it a quick shake. "Deal."

Chapter Ten

The next afternoon was Wednesday, two days before the meet. Grace sat with Jaci at the snack bar. They were both eating soft, swirly ice cream cones, the perfect thing on a sultry July day. After a brief break in the heat wave, the temperature was back above ninety degrees, and all the pools were crowded with recreational swimmers.

"There's Jordan," said Jaci, gesturing toward the teen-age lifeguard sitting high in his chair, watching the water carefully. "I can't decide if he or that other lifeguard, Brad Baudinet, is more handsome."

"That other lifeguard, Chad what's-his-name, is pretty hot too," said Grace with a giggle.

"I saw the three of them sitting in the lifeguard lounge

yesterday on their break," said Jaci. "It was like looking at a beautiful painting or something."

"Stick with Jasper," said Grace. "He's more your type anyway."

"I know. It's true. And what about you and Justin? Do you like him?"

"Kind of, I think. But I kind of still like Mike."

Jaci rolled her eyes. "I think I'm going to break my own rule and completely submerge myself in the water." She set down her ice cream, which she'd licked down to the cone.

"Don't do anything too radical now," admonished Grace with a grin.

"Well, even I have my limits as to how much heat I can tolerate. And it's just too darn hot not to submerge my body."

Sunlight glinted off the water. A bee buzzed around someone's abandoned soda can at the next table. Jaci stood up. Her oversize T-shirt depicted a cat hanging from a tree branch with a slogan in sparkly letters that said "Hang in There." She peeled it off and headed for the pool. "Look. There's Jen Cho," said Jaci over her shoulder.

Grace gave a start and looked. Jen was talking to Coach Dana, leaning glumly on her crutches and nodding at whatever Dana was saying to her. Her leg was no longer in the detachable Velcro strappy thing Grace had last seen on her. Now it was encased up to the knee in a hard cast. Grace's heart sank. *How awful that must feel on such a hot day,* she thought.

Jen sat down in a chair and Dana moved another chair over so she could prop up her leg. Then Dana left. *It's now or never,* Grace thought.

"Hi, Jen. Can I talk to you?" asked Grace.

"Hi, Grace. Sure. Sit."

Grace sat. "How is your leg?"

Jen grimaced. "Itchy and achy, to tell you the truth," she said.

Grace nodded. She swallowed. "Listen, Jen. I want to tell you something and I hope you don't get too mad at me, although I won't blame you if you do."

Jen's eyes widened. She shifted in her chair and waited for Grace to continue.

"See, the day you slipped? I'd been making a picture out of sunblock, tracing it right on the tile like finger painting. It was dumb, I know. And I didn't clean it up very well. And you slipped on the slippery part and hurt yourself and so it's my fault." Grace couldn't look at Jen. The words just tumbled out of her.

"Grace."

"I know, it was so bad of me not to—"

"Grace!"

"What?"

"You didn't cause my accident."

"But yes, I did! The place where you wiped out was—"

"I didn't wipe out. I *fainted*."

"You . . . fainted?"

"Yes. I've been doing that for a while now. My doctor says I have low blood pressure, so sometimes if I haven't had enough water, I get dehydrated, which makes me really dizzy, and sometimes when I stand up I completely pass out. The day of the picnic I'd been swimming all day and you remember how hot it was, right? I remember thinking I should go get some water, and then the next thing I knew I was on the ground and my leg really hurt. I didn't slip. I promise."

"Oh." Relief flooded through Grace.

"So all this time you've been feeling guilty? You've been thinking everything was your fault?" She laughed. "You should have said something before."

Grace nodded. She had a big lump in her throat and her eyes felt hot. She didn't want to cry.

"The doctor says it's just a simple fracture, and actually, fractures can be less complicated than bad sprains. I'll be out of this cast in a few weeks and back in the pool rehabbing. It stinks to miss the season, but there are things they let me do to keep in shape."

"That's nice," said Grace.

"Actually, I'm doing some stuff this summer I wouldn't have had time to do if I'd been swimming competitively, like going to this really cool robotics camp."

Grace nodded again, and this time she managed a smile.

"But you still have to beat Fair Isle in the relay on Friday for me," said Jen. "I'll be there to cheer you on."

Grace stood up and gave Jen a hug. "I feel so much better now! I'm going to go practice my starts!"

"That's the spirit!" said Jen. "Now go out there and win for me!"

Chapter Eleven

"Coach Dana? Can I talk to you for a minute?" asked Christina.

"Sure, Christina. What's up? You look upset. Is something wrong?"

Christina had been waiting for Coach Dana to appear, and as soon as Dana had left Jen's table, Christina hurried over to intercept her near the snack bar.

"Um, can we sit down?"

Coach Dana nodded and steered her toward a table under a shady umbrella. They sat.

"I wanted to tell you that I'm sorry about the fight you had with Coach Paul," Christina said in a small voice.

"Oh, that," scoffed Dana. "It's not a big deal. He just

caught me at a bad moment, that's all. I don't think he really meant too much harm by his dumb joke, but I have to say, it was pretty terrible timing for him to—"

"It wasn't him! It was me!" Christina blurted out. She was vaguely aware that Dana would probably be confused by her outburst, but she didn't care. She just needed to get the words out.

Dana blinked twice. "What are you talking about?"

Christina took a deep breath. "I took your phone. I went into your stuff and took it when no one was looking. Then I went over and hid it near Paul's backpack."

Dana sat back in her chair and stared at Christina. "Why on earth would you do something like that, Christina?"

"Because I, well, I was trying to get you two together."

"Me? And Paul?" Dana stared at her.

Christina had the weirdest feeling that Dana was somewhere between laughing and crying.

"And you thought you could do that by—by *stealing* my *phone*?"

"Well, it kind of backfired, but I just thought the two of you could make such a nice couple, and I thought maybe if you couldn't find your phone, he could help you find it, which is what did happen, but I didn't think it through and it looked like he'd taken it on purpose. I thought maybe it could just seem like you'd lost it and he helped you find it and then you'd look at each other not as coaches but, you know, in a different way. You just seem like you'd be so cute together and now I've screwed everything up and made you hate each other and it's all my fault and I'm so, so, so sorry and you're probably going to fire me as the manager and I deserve that but—"

"Christina."

Christina darted a look at Dana's face and was startled to see a smile twitching at the corners of her mouth. Was she not mad?

"I get it. I'm not going to fire you. But"—here her face became stern again—"you need to go apologize to Coach Paul as well. I will too, of course, but really, you need to explain to him what you did and why."

Christina nodded glumly. She knew Coach Dana was right, but she dreaded having to face Coach Paul. She barely knew him. "So you're not mad?" she asked Dana.

Dana chuckled. "Maybe a little. But you meant well." She crossed her arms and shook her head. "Paul and I could never—" She stopped talking. "It just wouldn't work, trust me. But I appreciate your trying."

"I really thought you guys would be a good couple," said Christina sadly.

A funny look came into Dana's eyes, sort of a combination of sadness and . . . something else that Christina couldn't understand. "We're both in college," said Dana. "We've known each other for years, but we go to schools that are hundreds of miles apart. It's absurd to think about."

Christina nodded and stood up. "I'll go find Coach Paul," she said. "I'm so glad you're not too mad."

"No, I'm not mad. But my contact is acting up, so you better go," said Dana, and she hurried toward the locker room, a tissue pressed to the corner of her eye.

"So she knows I didn't take her phone?" asked Paul after Christina had explained and apologized over and over again. "She's not angry with me anymore?"

"No. She just said I should apologize to you," answered Christina.

"Did she think it was a crazy idea?"

"What?"

"You know, your idea. Of us. Dana and me." He looked anxiously into Christina's eyes.

"Oh, that. Yeah, she said it was out of the question because you guys went to colleges that were really far away from each other," said Christina.

Paul wilted a little and nodded. “Yeah, she’s right. It’s crazy.”

Christina’s internal radar began to beep. *Hmmm,* she thought. *Hmmm.*

Chapter Twelve

"So, how did it go?" asked Grace a little while later. She and Christina were wading side by side in the shallow end of the T-shaped pool, leaning back on the wide steps.

"Better than I expected," said Christina. "She was a little mad at first, but then she seemed to understand. And Coach Paul was nice about it too. He seemed really interested in finding out what Coach Dana thought about the whole thing. I think maybe, just maybe, they might like each other."

Grace shook her head and grinned. *There she goes again,* she thought.

"How did it go with Jen?" asked Christina.

"Pretty well," said Grace. She told Christina all about

the conversation she'd had with Jen.

"Oh, you must be so relieved," said Christina.

"Yeah," agreed Grace.

"I remember seeing you sitting there that day. Who were you drawing a picture of, anyway?"

Grace mumbled something Christina couldn't hear.

"Who?"

"Mike. Justin asked me to."

"Oh. So you were totally flirting with two guys at the same time."

Grace frowned. "No, I wasn't. Not really. I was just drawing a picture. Justin *asked* me to."

Christina snorted and then said, "Could've fooled me. You've been spending a lot of time with both those guys, I've noticed."

"They've been helping me with my butterfly stroke!" sputtered Grace.

Christina made air quotes. "'Helping.' Uh-huh."

Grace turned toward Christina and sat up. "Well, at least I'm not spending every waking hour thinking about who's popular, and what's in fashion, and who likes who, and trying to get *old* people together!"

"*Old*? You mean the coaches?"

"Yeah, I mean the coaches."

"Well, maybe if you spent one second thinking about others instead of yourself—"

"That's not fair!"

"That day Jen hurt herself, you didn't even bother to come over to see if she was okay."

"I was scared! I thought it was my fault!"

"And every time I see you, you're sitting around with Mike, flirting or talking or swimming with him or whatever. You told me you would ask him about me. I've liked him since that day I saw him in the mall! But obviously you like him yourself!" Christina shot back, her eyes flashing.

Suddenly both girls noticed that several people who'd been splashing around in the pool had stopped and were staring at them.

"I have to go," said Christina. She stood up and splashed up the stairs.

Grace didn't even say good-bye to her. She just sat there fuming.

Chapter Thirteen

Grace stood in the midst of a huddle of three other girls and Coach Dana, just before the start of the very first event of the day. Their heads were bowed together. Despite her nervousness, Grace loved the feeling of being part of the "elite" team. She loved the crimson-colored racing suits with the gold diagonal stripe, and even though she hated wearing one, she loved the look of the crimson bathing caps with the letters RSC written out in gold. Lisa, Veronica, and Nandini looked as excited as she did—but she was positive they were not as terrified. She knew both her parents were somewhere in the crowd, but it was just as well that she hadn't spotted them. All she needed was to see her dad in his dumb hat, with his dumb camera pointed at her. Parents could be so mortifying.

"Just remember to do what we did in practice," said Coach Dana. "Veronica, arch your back on your start. Lisa, think long and strong on the freestyle—long arms, strong kicks, just as you've been doing all week. Nandini, shorten your glide time the way we discussed. And Grace—remember not to breathe when you're going into the turn. And keep those thumbs pointed down. And don't tuck your head too much."

"Let's win this for Jen!" said Veronica.

"For Jen!" everyone else chimed in.

They'd had several meets already this summer, but this one was by far the biggest and the first one Grace was really competing in. Five other teams had come to compete, both boys and girls. The meet was being held at RSC because of its two pools. Swimming and diving could be run at the same time. Grace had never seen so many swimmers in one place before. The RSC kids had staked out their area on the pool deck, a sea of gold and crimson amid all the other bright-colored suits and caps.

Grace turned and looked for Jen. There she was, leaning on her crutches and wearing an RSC T-shirt and sweats, surrounded by their teammates. She heard the announcer call for the girls' medley relay event. RSC would be in lane three, and Fair Isle in lane two. Veronica, Celine from Fair Isle, and the rest of the backstroke swimmers jumped into the water so they could assume the position for the start. Veronica was good at backstroke, but Grace couldn't help but notice how powerful and strong some of the girls in the other lanes looked. She didn't dare scan the crowd to see if Justin or Mike were watching. Mike was the anchor in his own medley relay, so most likely he was off stretching somewhere.

The backstrokers got in the ready position. Grace couldn't see anything except their heads, but she knew their hands were grabbing the handles underneath the starting block, their legs bent, their feet flat against the wall. When the starter called, "Take your mark!" they all moved their bodies almost completely out of the water, coiled up and poised to spring backward. Grace held her breath. The announcer called, "Ready!" and then the buzzer sounded.

As the spectators roared and cheered, Veronica sprang backward, throwing her head back and arching her body, her arms out in a T position and then reaching for the water. It was a good start. But two of the other girls—Celine in lane two and another girl in lane six—had good starts too. The girls in those three lanes swam underwater in a rapid dolphin kick, and then three heads emerged as the leaders broke into a full backstroke.

It was still neck and neck at the wall, but Veronica lost some time on her turn. RSC assumed third place as the swimmers approached the girls waiting on the blocks. Fair Isle had taken the lead.

When Veronica touched the wall, Grace's team was still in third place, and the fourth-place team was closing the gap. *Splash. Splash.* And then a third *splash* as Nandini dove in, a good dive. One pull, one kick-glide, and then her head emerged from the water and she began her breaststroke. Was she gaining on the girl in lane six? Grace's heart pounded as she stepped onto the starting block. As Nandini came into the wall, she seemed to gain on the girl, but once they had turned and their heads emerged, Grace saw with a sinking feeling that Nandini was still in third place, behind lanes two and six, and the fourth-place girl was gaining on her.

Grace crouched over the block, her head tucked, waiting for Nandini to touch the wall. Out of the corner of her eye she saw one girl, then another, dive into the water. Then it was her turn. As Nandini stretched for the wall, Grace dove in, trying to remember everything Coach Dana and Justin had told her. She imagined she was diving over the noodle. It was a clean entry. She whipped her lower body in a dolphin kick. But as soon as she emerged from the water and began her stroke, she put Dana and Justin out of her thoughts, and her body seemed to move automatically, with no orders from her brain. Before she knew it, she was approaching the wall. Had she gained on the leaders? She didn't dare spare the time to look. She leaned toward it, touched it with both hands, let her feet come underneath her, and then threw her right arm over her head and exploded off the wall. She immediately went into her dolphin kick underwater, but remembered to emerge in time so she wouldn't get disqualified.

Now it was a sprint to the wall. She had no idea where swimmers were in the other lanes—the water churned all around her, white and foamy. Her lungs burned—she didn't even know if she was taking the time to breathe—and her arms ached, but she concentrated only on touching the wall. As she did she could sense Lisa leaping over her and landing in the water behind her, freestyle stroking her way through the last leg of the relay. As Grace's head popped out of the water, she could hear loud cheering. She climbed out. Coach Dana clapped her on the back. "You got us back to second place!" she shouted over the cheering and clapping. Then Jen was there too, giving her a big hug, not minding that Grace was soaking wet.

Grace, Dana, and Jen turned to watch Lisa's leg of the medley. Lisa had caught up with the Fair Isle girl in lane two! There were fifteen yards to go. With a sudden burst of speed, Lisa shot forward and touched the wall a fraction of a second before the other girl did. They'd won!

The four girls threw their arms around one another and jumped up and down as though they were all on a trampoline, then pulled Jen into the mix and hugged her, too. But Grace barely had time to celebrate when she felt someone tapping her shoulder. It was Christina.

"You have to go over to the diving area!" said Christina. "You're almost up!"

Grace's jaw dropped. "I am? I thought boys were going right now!"

"No time to talk," said Christina, pulling Grace from the group and giving her a little shove toward the diving platforms. "Boys and girls got switched, and you've been moved up in the diving order."

Grace was still panting and exhausted from her race, but she wasn't about to miss her turn. She hurried as fast as she could—without running, of course—over to the diving area. The first dive wouldn't be so bad, she knew. It was a simple forward dive in a tuck position. She'd practiced it a million times. She approached the diving area just as her name was being called.

"Grace Davis," said the announcer. "Forward dive in a straight position. Degree of difficulty: one point four."

Grace climbed onto the one-meter platform. Suddenly she froze. *That isn't the dive I wrote on my dive sheet!* Her first dive was supposed to be a forward dive tuck, not a forward dive *straight*! What had happened? She looked for Coach Michelle, but she didn't see her. Anyway, it was too late now. She had to concentrate. She knew she could do this—it wasn't a difficult dive. But distracting thoughts kept crowding into her head. How could she have written it wrong? And had Coach Michelle approved it? She was still out of breath from the relay! Never mind, she told herself. If she failed this dive she'd get a zero for the team, and she wasn't going to do that.

Stop. Breathe. Go.

She began her approach. With a powerful jump straight up, she circled her arms above her head, jumped high, then laid out and entered the water. But it wasn't a clean entry. She knew her toes weren't pointed, and then the backs of her calves slammed the water.

Ouch! she thought as she plunged down into the Blue World, the muffled place where she felt so safe.

Her head popped up and she shook the water from her eyes so she could see the judges' numbers: all 2s and 3s. Ugh. She'd have to do better than that. She climbed out of the water and grabbed her chamois to dry off. The backs of her calves stung. For her next dive she'd be prepared.

"Grace Davis," said the announcer. "Reverse one-and-a-half in a tuck position. Degree of difficulty: two point one."

Grace walked toward the board. Her previous four dives had been the ones she'd expected, and she'd done pretty well. This would be her sixth, last, and hardest dive. But Grace was ready.

She started her approach, then attacked the board, jumping high into the air, throwing her head backward, and tucking her knees as her body rotated once and then again. She spotted the water and reached for it, her body fully extended, and sliced into the water, down into the quiet blue, bubbles whooshing past her ears. She knew it had been a good dive.

And it was. When she popped up, the scores were already flashing. A 5, two 5.5s, and a 6! YESSSS!

Grace ended up getting fourth place overall in the

diving competition. Her parents came up to hug her and congratulate her.

"Oh, you were so wonderful, darling!" her mom gushed as her dad recorded this moment with his camera.

Grace knew they meant well. "Thanks," she said, gently extricating herself from her mom's hug. "Hey, I think they need some parents to help with the snack table," she said.

Her parents got the message. "All right, we'll go help," said her mother.

"Grace did a great job today," said Coach Michelle to Grace's parents as they were heading away. "She has gained so much confidence in her abilities in the past few weeks."

Grace smiled to herself as she packed up her stuff. Fourth place was pretty good, considering it was her first major competition. The two Fair Isle girls had gotten first and second place, and Grace had heard that the third-place girl had been diving for years. *If only I'd had more time to recover after the relay,* she thought ruefully. *And if only there hadn't been that mix-up about my first dive. That was definitely weird.*

Michelle came over and patted her shoulder. "You really nailed your last dive. If you keep it up, and practice hard, you could become a truly spectacular diver," she said.

"Thanks," said Grace. All in all, Grace really did feel proud of herself. She'd helped her team beat the other teams—including Fair Isle—in the relay. She'd never been in such a high-stakes competitive race before, and she hadn't choked! And Coach Michelle had just complimented her.

Michelle moved off to talk to some other divers, and Grace found herself standing next to Mike. For once she didn't immediately clench up with nervousness in his presence. Was she getting better at overcoming her shyness?

"Hey, nice job today," said Mike. "I heard your relay got first place."

"Thanks," said Grace. "How did you do?"

"Two firsts, including a first in the individual medley. We came in second in the medley relay," he said with a casual shrug.

"Wow, great," said Grace. "How did Justin do in the diving?"

Mike grinned. "He got fifth place overall, and he's pumped about it," he replied. "He says he owes it all to you!" With a dramatic swing of his arm, Mike offered his hand for Grace to shake.

She giggled and shook it. Then she looked around for

Justin. "I'll go congratulate him!" she said, spotting him near the snack bar.

"Good job today on your start!" Justin grinned as she approached.

"I pretended I was jumping over that stupid noodle," said Grace, smiling and hiding her braces out of habit. "Congratulations on your diving. I heard you did great."

"Thanks. I had a pretty bad belly flop in the reverse dive, but other than that I did okay. I heard you got fourth. That's awesome."

"It would have been nice if I'd had more time to rest between the medley and my first dive," said Grace, shaking her head. "And somehow I messed up my diving sheet and wrote the wrong first dive. But I'm happy about how I did."

They stood next to each other, silently watching the little kids splashing around in the pool. Grace realized she didn't mind the silence. It wasn't awkward, like she was trying to come up with something they could talk about. It felt comfortable. Had she changed, or was it Justin? She liked that he liked to talk about movies, and bugs, and sports. He had interests. She liked standing next to him. She didn't mind that they were practically the same height. Maybe she was a little taller, but who cared? *His feet were definitely three sizes bigger than hers,* she thought, looking down at his big sneakers. Suddenly everything about him seemed . . . cute. She wished Mel were here so she could tell her all about him. She'd definitely call her later that night.

Finally Justin spoke. "Looks like our coaches aren't too mad at each other anymore. That was quite an argument they had."

Grace followed his gaze. Dana, Paul, and Michelle were standing together and chatting, along with Michelle's husband, Ryan. Ryan was holding their baby, an adorable six-month-old boy named Jack. The baby wore a hat with flaps covering his ears and his neck and round baby sunglasses. Grace giggled. "Yeah, they seem to be talking to each other now, at least," she agreed. "I guess they realized it was just a big misunderstanding." She thought about her conversation with Christina and wondered—again—*what* Christina had been thinking when she came up with that scheme.

"So, you want to get some fries or something?" asked Justin. "Smells like Marty just made a fresh batch. My dad gave me some money this morning, so I'm feeling loaded today."

Grace smiled again, so widely that she couldn't hide her braces even if she wanted to. "Sounds great."

Chapter Fourteen

Later that afternoon, Christina and her dad pulled into RSC. Christina was holding a big bunch of flowers for Coach Dana. As she was about to get out of the car, she turned back to her dad.

"Thanks for understanding about the party, Dad," she said. "I know you had big plans for us to do something together tonight."

Her dad grinned. "A pool party on a beautiful summer night definitely trumps an evening with your old dad," he said. "Have fun. I'll pick you up at ten."

She got out and waved to her dad as he drove off. She was grateful that he understood how important it was for her to go to the pool party at RSC tonight, even though he'd expected her to spend the evening with him. He'd even given her some money to help pay for the flowers for Coach Dana, although she hadn't mentioned *why* she was giving her flowers. She was forced to admit that her dad seemed, well, nicer and more easygoing ever since he'd moved out of the house. Not that she wanted things this way, of course.

She sniffed the large bouquet wrapped in crinkly purple paper and cradled it in her arm. Coach Dana didn't seem *too* mad at her anymore, but she hoped these would help Coach Dana forgive her for her dumb idea. Maybe they could get back to where they'd been before the whole fiasco with Coach Paul happened.

It was not even five, with a lot of daylight still left, so hardly any of the older kids were there yet. Christina wondered what Mike had been thinking, agreeing to sell raffle tickets at such an early hour. He probably hadn't thought about it at all. Oh well. It was just an hour.

As Christina approached the party area, she gave a little gasp of delight. Someone had gone all out to decorate—Marty, maybe? Or maybe some of the super-involved swim-team parents she'd gotten to know. The place looked magical. Colorful paper lanterns were lit up within the snack-bar area, and someone had coiled strings of white lights around the trees and in the branches that hung over the tables. The lights would look awesome once darkness fell. A "DJ in a box" was set up near the larger pool, and all the lounge chairs had been cleared away to make room for dancing. Lots of younger kids were milling around; they'd probably be leaving soon, and then the fun part of the party would start.

Christina went to the clubhouse for the raffle tickets and money box, then set herself up at a table. She watched the kids running and playing, the parents chatting and eating. As it turned out, she sold a lot of raffle tickets during her shift. And when six o'clock rolled around, many of the older kids started showing up.

When her shift was over, Christina was free to get up and mill around. By now it had gotten pretty crowded, and the music was playing louder; a few brave kids had even started dancing. She looked around for Mike. Not here yet. There was Coach Paul, deep in conversation with Tom and Kyle, sitting on the starter blocks at the far end of the lap pool. She looked for Coach Dana. *Aha. There she is.* She looked like she'd just arrived. Hmmm. Her hair was down and floating around her shoulders in a way Christina had never seen it before. And she was wearing . . . a *skirt*? Christina watched her plunk her tote bag on a chair and then hurry over to chat with Jen Cho, who was still on crutches. Jen seemed cheerful and chatty tonight with all her teammates close by.

Christina picked up the bouquet of flowers and set off toward Dana. She would present them to her with another apology. But she stopped after one step. A new thought occurred to her. She looked at Dana, surrounded by swimmers. She looked over at Paul, still sitting on the blocks and talking with Tom and Kyle. She looked down again at the flowers. Quietly stepping over to an empty table, she opened her bag and pulled out a pen and a little note pad that she always kept handy. It would be a challenge to make her handwriting—usually rather girly, she had to admit—look more masculine, but she thought she could do it. Carefully she wrote: *Hope these flowers can help make it up to you. P.* Then she looked at her cell phone, checked out a phone number, and committed it to memory.

Dana's back was still turned to Christina as she tiptoed over to Dana's bag. Quickly she placed the flowers on top. She tucked the note inside the foliage where Dana would be sure to see it.

She knew, of course, what Paul's backpack looked like, and she hoped her hunch was right. It was. There was his trusty clipboard, which she'd almost never seen him without. Across the top of the stat sheet, Christina wrote the phone number along with *Feel free to call me sometime. D.*

That should do it, she thought, and snuck away before anyone noticed her.

Chapter Fifteen

Grace almost walked past Jaci without recognizing her. "Wow," she said. "You look amazing!"

Jaci grinned. "Go ahead, make fun."

"No, I'm serious! You did something to your hair, right?"

"I washed it," said Jaci drily.

She really does look pretty tonight, Grace thought. Jaci was one of those people who could transform from ugly duckling to swan quite dramatically. She had great features and was tall and slim, but she almost never paid one bit of attention to her clothes or her hair or anything. Grace admired Jaci's short, flippy, bright-green skirt and her almost Day-Glo pink T-shirt, which somehow worked perfectly together. And her hair was brushed and glossy and swingy.

"All right, if you must know, I let my mom and my aunt art-direct my outfit tonight," said Jaci. "I usually don't let them, but I heard Jasper was back from band camp and that he's coming with his brother, so I wanted to put my, ah, best face forward. Have you seen them around?"

"No, not yet," said Grace. She actually had looked for Jasper when she arrived, just after she'd scoped out the place for Justin. Neither were there yet.

"Actually, there they are, six o'clock," muttered Jaci, gesturing slightly with her chin. "Is my hair okay? Any of my clothes on inside out?"

Grace smiled. It was nice to see Jaci so downright giddy over a boy for once. "You look great."

Sure enough, Mike, Justin, and Justin's twin, Jasper, were walking into the snack-bar area. Jasper looked a lot like Justin, of course, but there was no confusing the two. Justin's hair was cut shorter and stuck out all over, whereas Jasper's was longer and seemed to have an easier time lying down across his head. Also, Grace noted, Jasper's khaki shorts and T-shirt looked as though they'd been ironed. *With a stark contrast to his twin,* she thought, whose clothes often resembled crumpled aluminum foil.

"Wish me luck," said Jaci, throwing back her head and squaring her shoulders.

"Good luck," Grace said as Jaci headed off in Jasper's direction.

As soon as Jaci had left, Christina strode over to talk to Grace. "Listen, I'm sorry about our fight," she said.

"Me too," mumbled Grace.

"I've seen you with Justin and I know you aren't interested in Mike 'that way.' Justin seems really, um, nice."

Grace shifted uncomfortably.

"So can you bring it up?" Christina asked.

Grace furrowed her brow. "Bring what up?"

Christina took a deep breath and then blew it out. "Me. Us. Me and Mike. Can you please ask him if he likes me?"

"Oh. Um. I have to find the right opportunity."

Christina's eyes narrowed. "Seems like the right opportunity is never going to come along. Every time I turn around I find you near Mike, talking and laughing and flirting and . . . well, whatever else you're doing with him!"

Grace stared at Christina, her eyes narrowing. "What's that supposed to mean? I don't know *what* you're talking about. I barely ever see him!"

"As if! You see Mike all the time. Admit it: you haven't asked him about me because you like him yourself!"

"That is so not . . . not really true," said Grace lamely.

Christina crossed her arms and glowered at Grace. "You can't throw yourself at two guys at the same time."

"I haven't done that! Anyway, you should talk. You like everyone. Last time I checked, you were all about Max Mosello. Now it's Mike. You can't just go around tagging every good-looking guy you see and announcing that no one else gets to like him in case you decide *you* do!"

"That is not fair!" Christina's voice had grown shrill. Her eyes were bright, and pink blotches appeared on her cheeks. "You know what? I'm *glad* I changed the order of the events," she said defiantly.

That made Grace pause. "What are you talking about?"

"In the meet. I had to move someone into the first diving slot, so I chose you because I was mad at you."

"And then you changed my dive, too?"

"What are you talking about?"

"On my dive sheet. I'd written down a forward dive tuck and *somebody* changed it to a forward dive straight! It was you, wasn't it?"

"I didn't change your dive."

"I don't believe you."

"You must have written it wrong on your dive sheet. All I did was copy over what people wrote."

Grace was about to say something back, but stopped. Maybe, just maybe, there was a possibility she herself had written the wrong dive. But she couldn't be sure.

Christina shrugged. "Think what you want, but I would never intentionally screw something up like that. That could have disqualified the team."

No, Grace thought. She definitely remembered writing down her dives, and she'd been really careful. "If you're capable of moving me up in the lineup, why should I believe that you didn't also change my dive?"

"Because it's the *truth*!"

The girls squared off. Grace was breathing hard. Christina had her arms crossed and her eyes narrowed.

"Hey, guys!" someone said cheerfully.

Chapter Sixteen

Both girls whirled around. Mike and Justin were standing right behind them.

Christina and Grace exchanged a look of horror. How much of their conversation had the boys heard?

"So did you see the coaches?" said Justin.

Mike was grinning and shaking his head.

Four pairs of eyes swiveled in the direction Justin was pointing. Coach Dana and Coach Paul were sitting together at a table for two. Their heads were bowed together and they were talking intently to each other. On the table between them were the flowers Christina had brought. Dana leaned back and laughed, and then Paul did too.

Justin whistled. "I guess they've patched things up."

"Yeah, definitely," agreed Mike.

"I can't believe Coach brought her flowers," said Justin. "I would not have thought he had that in him!"

Christina beamed.

"Hey, the coaches are calling us over," said Justin.

Coach Dana and Coach Paul stood up when the four of them approached their table.

"So," said Dana, crossing her arms and looking straight at Christina. "It seems Coach Paul brought me some flowers, but he doesn't actually recall doing so."

Grace, Justin, and Mike all looked at one another, baffled. Christina suddenly became very interested in an ant that was making its way across the patio.

"And it seems Dana wrote her phone number on my clipboard. And you know what's weird about that? She knows that I already know her phone number by heart," added Paul sternly. "Why would she do that, do you suppose?"

"Christina? Anything you want to say?" prompted Dana.

"Sorry," she whispered.

The other three kids turned to look at her.

"Yeah, I brought the flowers. I was going to give them to Coach Dana to apologize for what I did, but then I changed my mind and pretended they were from Coach Paul. Then

I, well, I wrote Dana's phone number on Paul's clipboard and pretended it was her handwriting." She turned to Dana. "Are you going to fire me?"

Christina could feel the other three kids staring at her. When she darted a glance up at them, she noticed that Justin's mouth was actually hanging open in astonishment. Then she glanced quickly at the coaches. They were . . . smiling!

"I think we should tell them," said Paul to Dana.

Dana gave him an "are you crazy?" look. But then she shrugged. "Okay," she said.

"See, guys, Dana and I had been dating for two years," said Paul.

Now Christina's mouth fell open. All four kids stared from Dana to Paul and back to Dana.

"But we broke up last week," added Dana.

"Because, well, it's complicated, see," said Paul.

"*I* broke up with *him*," Dana said quickly. "Because I thought it was too hard to maintain a long-distance relationship while we're both away at college."

Paul sighed heavily.

"But maybe I was wrong about that," said Dana.

Paul jerked his head toward Dana. His eyes lit up with hope.

"I've never been more miserable than I was this week," she said, and looked over at Paul with misty eyes.

Mike found a plastic bottle cap and kicked it, soccer-style, toward the garbage can across the patio. Justin seemed to have something in his throat, because he kept making weird throat-clearing noises.

Grace looked astonished.

Christina couldn't stop sighing and smiling. "See, I knew you guys were perfect for each other," she gushed.

"How come you didn't say anything to all of us?" Grace demanded.

"We just thought, well, it would be better not to bring up personal stuff with the teams," said Dana.

"But now I guess you guys know," said Paul with a chuckle. "Anyway, we're back to being friends now."

"More than friends!" Dana blurted out.

Now everyone stopped and looked at Dana, who blushed to the roots of her hair.

"Anyway, Christina, you're not fired," said Dana. "But stick to managing the team from now on, okay?"

"Okay," said Christina happily.

"Now, scram," said Paul. "They've started the music. We're going to go dance."

The four kids watched their coaches link arms and

walk over to the dance area.

Justin whistled. "Well, *that* explains a few things. No wonder he's been working us so hard this week. His heart was broken. Maybe now that you've gotten them back together he'll ease up on us a little."

"Wait, what does all this have to do with practice?" asked Mike, puzzled.

"Nothing, man. Never mind. Just keep concentrating on swimming like you always do," said Justin, patting his friend's shoulder.

Grace smiled. Someone turned up the music. A new song started. "This is my favorite song!" said Grace. She looked from Mike to Justin, then back to Mike, then back to Justin. "So you want to dance or something?" she said to Justin.

Justin grinned. "Sure," he said.

As the two of them headed out to the dance area, Grace turned and looked at Christina. The look in Grace's eyes seemed to be saying, "Go ahead. Ask him to dance." Was that a challenge?

Christina and Mike stood side by side. It had grown darker, and the party lights glittered and twinkled on the warm summer night. It was unbearably romantic. Christina decided to just say it. "So you want to dance, or what?"

Mike was startled. He shook his head. "I stink at dancing. Remember?"

Christina nodded. The two of them stood there watching other people dance. She saw Grace's way-too-serious friend Jaci dancing with Justin's twin brother. *They seem just right for each other,* she thought. She saw coaches Dana and Paul dancing slowly together as though they were listening to very different music from what was actually playing. They stared into each other's eyes and spoke softly into each other's ears. Christina sighed dreamily. How cute they were!

Then she saw Grace and Justin dancing in a big crowd of swim-team kids, looking like they were really having fun. Maybe this Grace-Justin matchup was a good thing. It could take Grace's mind off Mike. Christina couldn't imagine going out with someone shorter than she was, but Grace didn't seem to mind.

Grace had changed so much. As someone who used to be terrified to talk to a guy, she now seemed so confident. And so lucky.

Mike scuffed his feet and checked the time on his phone. "Uh, well, so, I guess I should get going. I'm pretty beat. I did a lot of racing today."

A lump rose in Christina's throat. He definitely did not

like her. "Okay," she said in a false-cheerful voice. "Good job today."

"Thanks," he said, and disappeared into the crowd.

The lump in Christina's throat seemed to grow larger. She could hardly swallow. The decorative lights all blurred together. When the summer started, she had felt so hopeful. And now it was practically half over, and she was miserable. Her parents were still living apart. Everything with Grace was terrible. And the guy she'd had a mad crush on for weeks barely seemed to know she was alive. What was wrong with her? Why was everything so awful all of a sudden?

"Um, you want to dance?" asked someone next to her.

She turned. It was Kyle, one of Mike's teammates, and the second-best-looking guy on the swim team, in her opinion. He was also a good dancer, she'd noticed. And he was taller than she was! She darted a look for Mike. Had he left yet? No, there he was, standing by the door, talking to Marty and Coach Paul. Maybe he'd notice her dancing with Kyle. Maybe he'd realize lots of other guys thought she was attractive. Maybe he'd get a tiny bit jealous! She vowed not to give up on Mike. Maybe there was still hope.

She smiled sweetly at Kyle. "Sure," she said. "I'd love to."

Ready for more?

Turn the page for an excerpt from the third book in the Pool Girls series,

Cool Down!

New bathing suit? Check.

Latest issue of *Rocker* magazine, to show that she was as hip as the next girl? Check.

Expensive new leather flip-flops that she'd conned Dad into buying for her, knowing Mom would say no? Check.

Hottest guy in the Western Hemisphere just outside, who might just possibly, finally, notice she was alive? Check. Christina smiled ruefully. Of course Mike was out there. He was on his zillionth lap of the day, no doubt.

Christina did a little twirl in front of the locker room mirror, since no one else was in there. Yes, she had to admit, she looked pretty good in her new metallic-silver tankini, and she was having a great hair day. She clicked on her phone for perhaps the seventeenth time that day to reread Veronica's text from last night:

I asked MM if he liked anyone. Don't be mad. He said maybe kind of sort of but he wasn't positive. Progress?

Christina sighed. It was hard to know where things stood with Mike Morris. He was definitely the Strong, Silent Type. But she considered Veronica's text a step in the right direction.

She opened her bag to put her phone away when it buzzed in her hand. She clicked on the message. It was from Veronica.

Bad news. Sit down before you read my next text.

Christina stared at the text and then slowly lowered herself down onto the bench as though it were a too-hot bath. She texted back:

OK. I'm sitting. What?

The phone buzzed almost immediately.

I'm out here on the pool deck and so is MM. He's brought a friend. A girl.

Christina blinked at the words on her phone screen. That couldn't be possible. Veronica must have it wrong. Yesterday Mike had asked her if she'd be out at the pool today. That was as close as he got to asking her if she wanted to hang out with him. Why would he show up with another girl? There had to be some reasonable explanation. She texted Veronica:

OK, thanks. I'll do some recon before I come out. C U soon.

She took a deep breath and stood up. Only one way to find out—she'd have to spy. In the bathroom area there was a high window, just to the left of the sinks, and it looked right out onto the pool. After peering under the stall doors to be double sure no one was in there, she brought a chair over and stepped onto it, stood up carefully, and leaned over so she could see out.

She didn't have a great view, but she could definitely

see at least a third of the pool. He wasn't in any of those lounge chairs. Knowing him, he'd be in the water. She waited. A minute later, a swimmer powered across the pool and came to a stop at the end. His shiny brown head popped up and he swept his wet hair out of his face. It was Mike. She would know those muscular arms anywhere. He was talking to someone out of her sight line. Now he was laughing. He usually didn't laugh that hard. Here came another swimmer, someone under the water. A head popped up, long blond hair, shining like diamonds in the bright sunlight. It was a girl. Christina watched as the girl dove back under the water, popped up right next to Mike, and tried to push him down into the water by his shoulders. Laughing again, he casually peeled her delicate hands off his shoulders and playfully shoved her to the side. Now they were both laughing.

She heard the door open in the other room. Someone was coming into the locker room. Christina scrambled down off the sink, hurried out of the bathroom area, and nearly ran smack into Grace Davis.

"Oh!" said Grace, taking a step back and regarding Christina. "Hi."

"Hi," said Christina. Her thoughts were whirling. Grace was the last person she felt like seeing at a time like this. After the big fight they'd had a few weeks ago, they'd barely nodded hello to each other since, and Christina was not exactly in the mood for idle chitchat with her right now.

"You okay?" asked Grace. "You look a little . . . upset."

"Oh, I'm fine," replied Christina.

Silence.

"Hi, Grace! Hi, Christina!" Kimmy came into the locker room with her little sister, Emily. Kimmy was one of the younger girls on the swim team. Emily looked about six. "Hey, Grace, congratulations on winning Best New Diver at the swim team banquet last week."

Grace smiled, her braces glinting. Christina wished for her sake she would go for a different band color than green. It just seemed so, well, childish.

"Thanks, Kimmy," said Grace. She shot Christina a look. Christina didn't care. She wasn't about to congratulate Grace. Grace's head was way too big already after all the praise she'd gotten for her diving talent this summer.

"So are you guys just hanging out together today?" asked Kimmy.

"No," said both girls at the same time.

"I'm meeting Veronica here," said Christina. "She's leaving for vacation in a couple of days. Along with the rest of the universe," she added bitterly. It was true. Besides Grace, Christina felt like the last girl on earth not to be on vacation. Everyone was away. She'd been getting giddy text messages from both Ashley and Lindsay, her friends from school, who were at their respective fabulous beach houses and seemed to be having the best summers of their lives. It hadn't been so bad when she'd thought she might have Mike Morris to spend quality time with. But now everything looked bleak. And even Grace had more of a life than she did—she always seemed to be with her sort-of boyfriend, Justin.

"I'm looking after Emily," said Kimmy, rolling her eyes. "Come on, you. Let's get changed. See you guys." Kimmy proceeded into the dressing area with her sister.

Grace and Christina stood there awkwardly. Finally Grace spoke. "Justin and I are working on some new dives today."

Christina nodded, but she couldn't come up with anything to say about diving. More silence. "Well, guess I'll be going," said Christina, turning to leave.

Veronica burst into the locker room. "So did you see her?" she asked Christina, then noticed Grace. "Oh! Hey, Grace! I didn't know you were here! Congratulations again on your award!"

Grace smiled. "Hey, Veronica. Thanks. Congratulations to you, too. I think our winning the medley relay might just be one of the high points of my life so far. Who are you talking about?"

Christina cringed inwardly. Grace could be so annoying sometimes. Couldn't she see that this might be a private conversation between her and Veronica?

"Mike Morris showed up with a superpretty girl," said Veronica to Grace. "They're in the pool together right now. I've never seen the guy look like he's having this much fun." She darted a glance at Christina, as though she just realized what she'd said might have been insensitive. "Sorry. I just meant . . ."

"It's okay," said Christina. "Whatever. I'll be out there soon."

"Okay, see you out there," said Veronica. As she opened the locker room door, she turned back to address Grace. "Hey, Grace. My dad is letting me treat my friends—what's left of them not on vacation, that is—to lunch at the snack bar tomorrow. Are you around? We can have all the curly fries we can eat!"

Grace looked thrilled. "Sure!" she said. "I'd love to."

"Great," said Veronica. "Feel free to invite Justin if you want."

Grace smiled gratefully. "Thanks, that's nice of you. I'll ask him." She flung her bag over her shoulder and headed outside. Christina felt relieved. Now it was time for her and Veronica to scope out the Mike situation together.

Growing up, Cassie Waters spent every waking moment of every summer at her swim club (which was conveniently located at the end of her street). These days Cassie lives in the suburbs of New Jersey, writing and editing books, hanging out with friends, and having lots of fun. Over the years, Cassie has written dozens of books, but the Pool Girls series is nearest and dearest to her heart. She doesn't make it to the pool nearly as often as she would like these days, but she is still very good friends with the girls she used to hang out with at her swim club.

Ready for more drama?
Read all about the confessions of
Madison Hays in

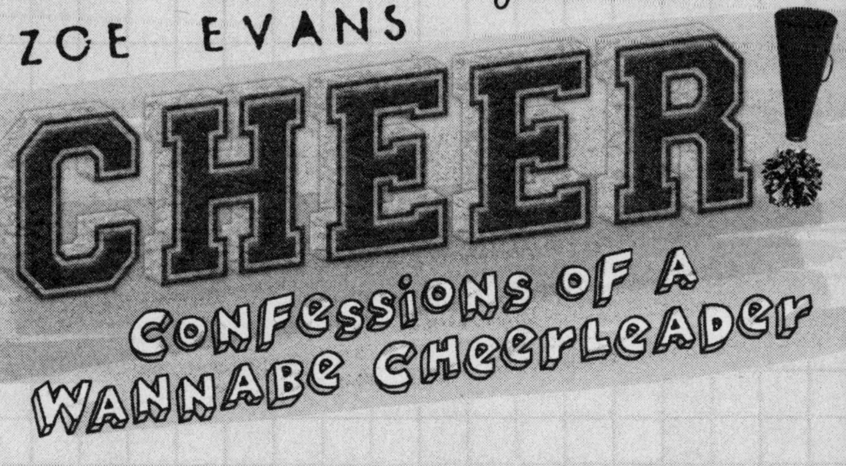

Turn the page for a sneak peek!

Saturday, September 4

Post Tryouts for the Titans, Port Angeles School parking lot

Spirit Level:

Bottom of the Pyramid

"Maaads." Mom cooed into my ear, shaking a pom-pom under my nose at the same time. This is how she's been waking me up every day since I was, like, three. And it's the same pom-pom. Between you and me, it's lost a few strings since its heyday and is starting to look really sad. "Big day today," she trilled. "Up! Up! Up!"

I opened my eyes and threw off the covers in ÜBERFREAKOUT mode. "What time is it? Am I late?" I scrambled toward my dresser to grab my contacts case. Not much gets me up on a Saturday with this much enthusiasm. Not much, that is, except the idea of tryouts for the Port Angeles School Titan cheerleaders. (OK, that and maybe the Farmers' Breakfast Special at the Pancake

House around the corner.) Trust me, it is THAT GOOD.

But back to why I was so excited about cheer tryouts. To start, a list of my favorite fun facts about cheerleading:

1) 3% of all female school athletes across the country are cheerleaders. Who knew?

2) 65% of all dangerous injuries in girls' school sports come from cheerleading. Insane!

3) 62% of cheerleaders are involved in a second sport. Overachievers much?

4) The first cheerleaders were men! Can you believe??

Mom was halfway inside my closet, selecting one of my red and white pairs of boy shorts and a tank (our school colors are red, white, and blue—patriotic much?) for me to wear to the tryouts. This is another one of our traditions—anything regarding cheerleading, Mom's allowed to help pick out my clothes. Every other occasion is off limits ever since I learned to use a sewing machine and discovered I have quite a killer fashion sense. And also, um, since I'm not five anymore.

"Madington, of course we're not late," she said, using a nickname I've warned her never to use when my friends are around. "We're an hour earlier than planned. Thought you'd want some time to digest the special whole-wheat pancakes I made you. I even put in some carob chips." She winked. "See you downstairs."

Mom laid my clothes on the bed and cheerily bounced out of my room, her wavy blond locks trailing behind her like a mermaid underwater. God, I L-O-V-E her hair.

Now might be a good time to mention that my mom is, like, absolutely gorgeous. I'm talking royalty pretty. No, seriously, she actually was homecoming queen **AND** prom queen in her day. Whenever she picks me up from school, I can always count on some guy or another to serenade us with that song "Stacy's Mom" that was popular a while back. They just substitute my name instead: "Maddy's mom has got it goin' on," and I just want to disappear in the front seat.

Oh, yeah. And she was a Titan. And she was captain

of the cheerleading squad.

You could almost say my mom and I have been preparing me for today's tryouts ever since I was old enough to wear her cheer uniform. Well, I didn't exactly fit into it. I was only three, and it dragged on the floor behind me, but I was technically wearing it. Every summer, while my friends were either lazing away at camp or catching up on the latest comic books, I was at cheer clinics, taking dance classes or tumbling and stunting lessons, dreaming of the day I'd make it onto the squad just like my mom. Which is why today's tryouts were, like, everything I've been living for my **WHOLE LIFE**! I'm pretty good at this cheer stuff too. That is, when I'm not being Spazzmadstic, which is what my mom and I call it when I get all awkward and mess up my moves.

Ok, so I guess I didn't get my mom's perfect cheer genes.

I also didn't get her model looks. I mean, I'm not saying that small children should be shielded from looking at me! I'm not hideous or anything, but no guy has ever told me I'm pretty, except for my friend Evan—but we were five at the time and he was picking his nose while he said it, so I'm not entirely sure that counts. Five foot three is a totally average height for a girl my age, and my eyes are this really cool light green, which is pretty rare. My wavy brown hair? That I wouldn't mind changing up. Eduardo, the guy who cuts Mom's and my hair, says my hair is "honey colored," like that's supposed to make me like it more, but I don't see much of a difference between the color of my hair and the color of the wood floor in our den, and I still totally wish Mom would let me dye it something dramatic like red or black. But she won't. I do like my freckles, though—and they really come out right before cheer season, because that's when I'm practicing outside the most (obvs).

In the car on the way to school, I selected some pump-it-up music on my iPod to get me psyched and to calm my nerves a little.

"Mads, turn it down. Even *I* can hear it," Mom said in that disapproving parental tone.

I pretended to turn the music down by rubbing my hands in the general direction of my iPod. This is a great thing about the older generation, as I like to refer to them. They don't know the first thing about how to operate anything with "pod" or "pad" or "i" in its name. Mom still has this giant tower of CDs in our living room, plus big fat books of CD collections. I keep telling her that CDs are so 1997, but she won't listen to me. Anyway, I don't ever have to worry about Mom snooping in my iPhone or (one day, hopefully, when I get one) my iPad. Not like she would, though. She's chill about those kinds of things.

Anyway, I started to think about what it would be like to make it onto the team. How amazing it would be to walk down the halls of PAS as a bona fide Titan, with peeps like Katie Parker, Hilary Cho, and Clementine Prescott having my back. I mean, they're not the nicest people in the world, but I don't think they're as bad as everyone thinks they are. People don't understand the kind of pressure they're under—giving every ounce of their physical strength to cheer on the Titans, not to mention all those supergrueling cheer competitions. It's enough to make someone lose it.

I mean, it's not like I want to be all besties with them. But to learn from the best cheerleaders? To earn respect from the best? To **BE** the best? **THAT** I can totally see. And I would so love to wear that white, red, and blue skirt. It's adorbs.

"Madington, we're here."

It was weird. . . . Mom's voice sounded like it was coming from so far away. I hate being woken from perfect daydreams. Especially when the reality was that cheer tryouts were just minutes away. Hello, butterflies?

"You're going to be fabulous," she said, giving my arm a squeeze.

The gym smelled—as usual—like the bottom of an old Crayola box mixed with armpit sweat. Delish! I tried to tell myself that I was ready. I had my journal in my silver and gold gym bag for inspiration (with all my notes on cheers, stunt sequences, routines, and general thoughts on life—oh, and my fashion designs ☺), and not a single lump stood out in my ponytail. Whatever Katie and Clementine threw my way, I could handle. Right?

Hmm, well, maybe not.

As soon as I saw the other girls, aka the competition, stretching out on the mats, I got a little nervous. There was Katarina Tarasov, the Russian exchange student I'd heard about. She just started school with us this year. I heard she was practically Olympics material back wherever she was from.

I watched her practicing perfectly arched backflips across the mat.

"Hey, nice job," I told her as I walked by.

"You're welcome!" she said, smiling proudly.

Unfortunately she doesn't speak much English. I decided to avoid sharing mat space with her that morning. I didn't feel like teaching an Introduction to English class in addition to trying out.

"All right, girls," said Coach Whipley. (Isn't it funny how coaches always tend to have the most appropriate names?) "It's gonna go like this. Katie and Hilary are going to lead you through a dance routine. Then Clementine will teach you a cheer. Then you'll perform each as a group. The last part of tryouts will be individual tumbling and gymnastics. Clear?"

It was exactly what I had planned for. No curveballs. Phew.

The routine was set to a medley of songs by Rihanna, Pink, and Lady Gaga. Unfortunately, I had stuck myself next to Jared "It's Showtime!" Handler, whose interpretation of every move was sprinkled with outrageous jazz hands and Fred Astaire footwork. I couldn't believe he actually showed up for tryouts. I'd heard him telling everyone he was going to go for cheer this year when he didn't get any lead roles in last spring's <u>West Side Story</u>. I'd secretly been hoping he was joking. Not that I mind people going for new things, but I don't like that he's just using cheer to give him an edge for drama class.

All through the dance routine, led by the amazing Hilary, Jared kept bumping into me and ruining my already-compromised-on-a-regular-day rhythm. I was so worried he was going to accidentally slap me with those jazz hands that I kept flinching. I missed a couple of steps in the middle of the routine and messed up a turn that normally would have been fine for me if I'd been able to concentrate fully. I looked like I was being electrocuted!! I swear, at next year's <u>Once Upon a Mattress</u> production I'm going to sit in the front row on opening night and rap Eminem while Jared sings lead.

I totally aced the cheer, but during the individual tumbling and jumping in front of the judges, I became Awkward Girl and seriously SpazzMadsed out. I accidentally hit my toe to my nose during a toe jump and even saw Clementine snicker. My triple backflip became a back **FLOP** in the last second because my hand caught on a weird piece of the mat (just my luck). By that time I had, like, zero confidence, so when the judges asked me to do a front handspring I didn't get enough height off the ground and **FREAKED** in midair, folding into a tumble instead. At this point, everyone was watching me in stunned silence. Like, the **WHOLE GYM**. I don't think anyone has ever had a worse cheer tryout. Even poor old Tabitha Sue Stevens—who can't even do a split (a regular one, like, on the floor)—looked sorry for me.

"That was . . . interesting. Thank you, Madison Hays," said Coach Whipley. And her face was all "what a loser," I could tell. I seriously wanted to burrow into the mat and just die. All that work, all those summers, for nada. My mom would be sooooo disappointed.

We weren't allowed to leave the gym until all the tryouts were over, so I suffered through the rest of the morning watching everyone else do way better than me and pictured my soon-to-be cheerless existence. I'd spend the rest of my life being a cheer wannabe. I'd probably end up a crazy old lady, still wearing her cheer uniform and grumbling, "I could have been something!" And when I died, people would feel sorry for me and bury me with my pom-poms.

"No!" I shouted.

"Huh?" grunted Jacqueline Sawyer, one of the Titan cheerleaders, who happened to be sitting near me.

"Oh, nothing." I blushed. I hadn't realized that I'd said that out loud. Sometimes I do that, though.

My daydreams can get pretty intense.

Jacqueline just looked at me like I had three heads. I figured I might as well get used to it, since that's how everyone will start looking at me after hearing I had the

WORST CHEERLEADING TRYOUT EVER.

"It's not that bad, you know," Jacqueline said, leaning in.

"What do you mean?" I asked. Was this chick reading my mind? Spoooooky.

"You'll still be cheering, just for a slightly different squad," Jacqueline said mysteriously.

Then it was my turn to look at her like she was from another planet. And then the realization hit me.

OH. NO.

The Grizzlies!!!

Jacqueline smirked and turned her attention back to the tryouts when she saw that I understood.

So, all the kids who don't make the Titans are automatically placed onto the Grizzlies, aka the B-squad, aka the rejects. I had completely forgotten about the school policy against turning anyone away from wanting to participate in school-spirit activities. The Grizzlies cheered for the school teams the Titans were too proud to cheer for: swim team, debate team, chess club, etc. In other words: Loserville! Last year, as a prank, some guys threw dog biscuits at the Grizzlies during a swim meet. Like I said, it's a world of **NO**. Love of cheerleading or not, I was **NOT** going to be a big, fat, hairy Grizzly.

I prayed that by some miracle my name would be on that magical sheet of paper outside Coach Whipley's office at the end of the day, securing my fate as a glorious and magnificent Titan.

Guess what? It wasn't. I must have stared at the paper, for like, ten minutes straight. I even tried walking away and quickly whipping around, hoping that my sneak attack would somehow shift the ink in my favor. It didn't work. My name was so **NOT** on there. Want to know where my name was? That's right. On the big, fat, hairy Grizzlies list! Sandwiched between Jared Handler and Tabitha Sue Stevens. Go figure.

Now all the new cheerleaders are running to their parents' cars, squealing with excitement. My heart can't sink any lower into my chest.

"I see you at the practice Monday, yes?"

I turned around and saw Katarina, her gym bag

draped over her thin shoulders. I just shrugged in reply. I wonder if she understood. Either way, if I AM going to see her at practice on Monday, I figure I can wait till then to start our English lessons.

Here comes my mom's car. Her expectant, smiling face is breaking my heart! What will she say when she finds out? She'll probably be mortified. This much I know is true: Pigs will fly before I become a Grizzly Bear.

I am meant to be a Titan.